"Hi, I'm Sarah."

The little girl held Jared's gaze with gray-green eyes. A wave of pain ripped through him; pain so intense it stole his breath. This child was a feminine replica of his brother. She had to be Mitch's daughter. Sarah was the secret Haley was hiding, the secret that may have cost his brother his life.

He watched the color drain from Haley's face. Like a bear protecting her young, she moved between him and Sarah, then Sarah skipped off to the barn.

"She's my brother's daughter, isn't she?" he asked when Sarah was out of earshot. The question nearly choked him. "What really happened the night Mitch died?"

SUSAN HORNICK

Susan Hornick lives in Colorado with her husband, two horses and a cat. As a child on her grandparents' farm, she loved creating stories in her head, which later translated into journals, short stories and finally novels. Her writing won numerous awards before finally finding a home in the inspirational market.

When not writing or spending time with her family, her biggest passion is visiting historical places—especially old cemeteries—and wilderness camping with her husband and friends, where she explores old ghost towns and wide open spaces from the back of her horse. Visit her on the Web at www.susanhornick.com.

More Than A Cowboy
Susan Hornick

Steeple
Hill®

Published by Steeple Hill Books™

STEEPLE HILL BOOKS

Steeple
Hill®

Recycling programs
for this product may
not exist in your area.

ISBN-13: 978-0-373-87510-8
ISBN-10:   0-373-87510-X

MORE THAN A COWBOY

www.SteepleHill.com

Printed in U.S.A.

Remember ye not the former things, neither consider the things of old.
Behold, I will do a new thing; now it shall spring forth; shall ye not know it? I will even make a way in the wilderness, and rivers in the desert.

—*Isaiah* 43:18–19

Deepest gratitude to Sharon, Pam, Janet, Kay, Robin, Peggy, Teresa, Alice and Heidi for their input. Also my husband, who relinquished "our time" so I could pound on the computer keys. And always, my children, Megan and Jon, who are as beautiful on the inside as they are on the outside, and my mom—who said "FINISH THE BOOK."

Chapter One

The rodeo announcer's voice blared over the loud-speaker signaling the day's final events for Cheyenne Frontier Days' rodeo competition. Haley Clayton wiped her sweaty brow and pushed through the crowd toward the bull pens lined up behind the arena.

A whistle from a nearby cowboy quickened her step. She ignored his slow perusal and moved on. The circuit consisted of mostly good, hardworking people with just a few rotten eggs. Today, the latter surfaced like bad pennies, stirring memories she'd locked away for eight years.

The chutes came into view. Haley dismissed her thoughts and focused on the pens. Several bulls bawled from a communal corral, but one stood alone, housed in a corner by thick steel panels.

Resurrection.

The bull that nearly killed her two years before. Haley's heart skipped, jarring a multitude of locked-up emotions. Fear rose from her core, reaching out to suffocate her like a boa squeezing the life from its next meal. The two thousand pound black Brahma fastened his eyes on her. He lifted his powerful head and sniffed the air, tossing his shorn horns as though they weighed a pittance, as though defying her to face him again. She edged closer.

"I remember you."

Her eyes closed briefly, trying to blot out the image of Resurrection's muscled fury battering her into the dirt, his foul breath blowing in her face as his massive head picked her up and tossed her across the arena.

"He looks impressive."

Haley jumped and spun around. The man towered over her like a lodgepole pine. Jet-black hair surrounded a face bronzed by wind and sun. Muscles rippled beneath the western shirt tucked neatly into a pair of Levis. Dark brown eyes scrutinized her with gentle humor and concern. Feminine appreciation stirred; then caution swamped her heart. He exuded power, and power was dangerous.

"He is," she said, stepping back. "You riding today?"

The man shook his head. "No. But my stepbrother is." He leaned against the rail. Resurrection snorted. "He's been away from the circuit for a few years putting his life back together. Sure would hate to see him make a comeback on that one."

Haley relaxed a little but kept a safe distance. She knew all about pulling her life back together. "Maybe he won't. There are a lot of bulls to draw from.

Chances are pretty slim to get this one. Besides, some of the best bullfighters in the country are in that arena to watch his back." The man's gaze shifted to rest on her. Haley shivered and broke eye contact.

"I hope you're right."

"Tell him to look fear in the eye and not let it defeat him."

Curiosity and interest lit his eyes. "You talk like you know something about the subject."

She did. In more ways than in the arena, but he couldn't know. She wanted to reach out and reassure him. Fear made her keep her distance. He glanced at his watch and smiled, revealing a set of perfect white teeth. Haley's chest squeezed.

"I'd better get back," he said. "Thanks for talking with me."

"You're welcome. Tell your brother we'll be watching out for him." The man disappeared around the corner.

Haley looked into Resurrection's eyes. "You won't win. I won't let you. I'll see you soon."

She forced her fear into the abyss from where it had risen. This bull was dangerous, unpredictable and as unreadable as a blank page. She would never underestimate him again.

She hurried to her camper parked beyond the grandstands, unlatched the door and flung it open. Her trailer held the July heat like a slow cooker. She opened the window and flipped the switch on the fan above the sink. The scents of popcorn, caramel and hot dogs oscillated in the breeze. Her stomach rumbled. If she hurried, she could make her costume change and still have time to see her daughter compete in the mutton busting competition.

Haley squeezed into the tiny bedroom she shared with Sarah and donned her clown outfit—ragged jeans, purple suspenders, a patched oversized shirt, and a red-and-blue wig topped with a round-rimmed polka dot hat.

Her father's picture rested in a wooden frame beside the bed. An identical costume covered his stocky body. His huge smile sported even white teeth surrounded by wide, painted red lips that stood out against the white face paint. A single black tear was painted near the corner of his eye.

Haley ran her finger over the glass, feeling his loss. Other pictures lined the wall. Pop holding Sarah in the hospital. Pop and Sarah blowing out birthday candles at two years and four. Then the last one—all of them together on Sarah's fifth birthday two years ago, a month before her crash with Resurrection that triggered his fatal heart attack. A soft knock outside drew her attention.

"Haley? You in there?" Hap Jenkins popped his head through the screen door.

"I'm here."

Haley set the picture aside and opened a jar of face paint, then glanced up. Her father's old sidekick leaned against the door jamb, resting his bum knee on the metal step. His gnarled hand gripped the bent aluminum frame that had seen better days.

"Sarah Rose sent me to fetch you," he said, staying in the doorway while Haley applied the face paint. "Mutton bustin'," he growled. "Kids ridin' sheep. Lot of foolishness if you ask me."

"I seem to remember you cheering me on when I was seven."

"Huh. Thought it was foolish then, too."

She met Hap's gaze in the mirror and slathered the white paint on her forehead. Would Hap and Pop have been so proud of her if they'd known the truth?

"How'd you fare in the competitions today?" Hap asked.

"I'm in the money. Top three for barrels. Should bring in a decent payback."

"How much more you need to buy that land?"

Haley tucked her hair under the wig, rose and stepped into the sunlight with Hap, closing the trailer door behind them. "A few more rodeos' worth. We can't keep traipsing around the country in this portable shack forever. Besides, Sarah wants to go to a real school this year."

She grabbed his arm and headed toward the sheep pens.

His feet shuffled in the dirt. "Resurrection's back."

She pulled her arm from Hap's, hoping he hadn't felt the tremor in her hand. "I know. I've seen him."

"Ain't too late to get someone else to take your place tonight."

Haley slowed her pace, letting Hap catch his breath. The pain, the months of recovery came back in a rush. She concealed her fear behind a forced shrug. "I figured I'd have to face him again someday or at least another like him."

"Ain't another bull like Resurrection."

She brushed her fingers across the costume fabric and felt the raised scars hidden beneath the shirt, constant reminders of her brush with death. "You blame Resurrection for Pop's heart attack," she murmured. "But he wasn't responsible."

"Mebbe not. But yer pop's old heart couldn't take seein' what that critter did to you. I couldn't take it either if…"

The sheep pens came into view. Hap's words trailed into a whisper. Haley stopped mid-stride and faced him, taking his rough hand in hers. He'd been like a second father to her. His feelings mattered.

"You always tell me to face what scares you most, stare it down and use it as a stepping stone." She smiled, hiding her fear under the surface. "Pop called it minimizing the monster without losing sight of the danger. No one thought I'd ever enter the arena again, Hap. But I did. I'll be fine."

"Them cowboys are depending on you to watch their backs."

"Keeping them out of the bulls' line of fire is my job. I'll do it." Haley spotted Sarah straddling the sheep pen fence and waved.

Sarah motioned them to hurry. Her gray-green

eyes sparkled with excitement. "Come on. Hurry. I'm next." She spun around and headed for the chute, her black braids slapping against her shoulders.

Haley leaned against the fence, gripping the rail. Her gut twisted every time Sarah rode. A few moments later a gate opened, releasing a black-faced sheep with a jean-clad seven-year-old clinging to its back like a monkey. The animal jumped forward, hunched its back, then sprinted. Haley held her breath as Sarah held on, then slid beneath the sheep's belly. Sarah picked herself out of the dirt. A smile hid her disappointment. Haley released the rail and wiped a bead of sweat from her cheek.

"Tough break," Hap called.

Sarah unpinned the number from her shirt and ran to the fence. "That was wild. Guess I'll be too old next year to compete. I'm going to miss it."

Haley hugged her daughter. "You did your best. That makes you a winner." She ruffled Sarah's bangs and flipped a braid. "Just think of all the new stuff you'll be eligible for next year, because you'll be 'old.'"

"Oh, Mom." The disappointment left Sarah's face.

Haley spotted Sarah's friends pulling their father through the gate. She handed Sarah the backpack stashed beside the fence. "The girls are here. Have fun at the sleepover. I'll see you tomorrow."

"Okay. I love you, Mom."

Haley gathered Sarah close. "I love you, too, Rosie girl." She planted a kiss on Sarah's head, leaving a streak of white face paint in the dark hair.

Sarah sprinted across the arena and disappeared. "I love you more than you know."

"She misses not having a father," Hap said, the old unasked questions sparking his eyes.

Haley clenched her fists. "I won't argue with you about this again, Hap. Especially not today. I'm going back to the pens."

"I take that as you don't want company."

"Maybe later," she said. "I need to concentrate on Resurrection."

"Ya might ask God for some help in that direction," Hap said.

"Praying never helped in the past."

Hap's sad smile added a few more wrinkles to his face. "Guess I still got enough prayers for us both. I'll check on the horses and see you later."

He limped toward the stables. Guilt replaced Haley's anger. Hap believed she was keeping Sarah from her father. But Hap didn't know the truth. No one knew. Except God. And the man who'd shattered her dreams. She wasn't faithless. She believed in God, just not in His ability to protect her or deliver the justice she felt she deserved.

The gift of Sarah didn't erase the violence of that one night or ease her sense of lost security and fear when a man showed too much interest. The handsome features of the man she'd met earlier popped into her mind. She quickly banished it. What she wanted she would never have. God had stolen her chance for a normal life. She couldn't rely on Him.

The truth will set you free. The phrase echoed in her mind, inviting confidences she neither asked for nor wanted. Spinning on her heels, she crossed the arena and hurried toward the bull pens. In a nearby booth, a radio played a familiar hymn. She hurried by before the music stirred memories of happier times, before the world had left its mark on her.

God could have changed the events leading to Sarah's conception. But He hadn't. It was she who had held the choice of life and death in her hands and had chosen life, and she would protect that life with her own, no matter what the cost. Sarah may not have been a product of love, but she was loved. And if God wouldn't protect the innocent, she would, even if it meant forever concealing the truth of Sarah's conception. Nothing—and no one—would ever hurt her daughter.

Jared Sinclair placed the last chair in the circle, then glanced at his watch. The small booth allotted to the Christian Cowboy's Fellowship didn't hold more than twenty people. That hadn't been a problem so far. Volunteering usually didn't take him away from his South Dakota ranch, but this trip was an exception. His stepbrother, Mitch Jessup, had asked him to come, and Jared arranged his schedule to combine business with spending some much needed time with Mitch.

Mitch's newfound faith was forged in the fires of trials, and Jared wasn't sure it was strong enough yet to handle a comeback into the life that had contributed so much to his downfall. He had to look out for Mitch, keep him centered and on track.

As if on cue, Mitch entered with a handful of old chorus books.

"I wish they hadn't rescheduled my ride. Do you think you'll be back from your business meeting in time to watch me?"

"Hope so," Jared said. "Who'd you draw?"

Mitch's square jaw tightened. "Resurrection. Great way to make a comeback, huh?"

Jared swallowed hard. A vision rose in his mind of the massive bull he'd seen earlier. Fear for Mitch closed his throat. "Maybe you should wait on this one."

"No. I'm ready. Besides, if I win, just think of the extra money I can donate to some worthy cause. I just wish…"

Jared waited.

"I just wish I hadn't wasted so many years."

"They aren't wasted if you allow God to use you with what you've learned," Jared said.

He helped Mitch arrange the music, an uneasy feeling dogging each movement. He'd hated what Mitch's hard drinking and womanizing had done not only to Mitch's body and soul, but to Jared's mother and Mitch's father.

But Jared had faithfully prayed for Mitch, and when his prayer was answered, Mitch was changed so completely that there was no doubt in anyone's mind that God did indeed answer prayer and transform lives. Still Jared sensed a hidden need—an unshared burden that weighed like a millstone around Mitch's neck.

"You made it back from the edge, Mitch. You can make a difference."

"What about the things I can't take back?" Mitch's voice filled with anguish. His gray-green eyes misted. "How do I make those right?"

Mitch's plea gnawed at Jared's gut. "Is there something you need to talk about?"

Mitch stared at the gravel floor. "I need to fix something, but I don't know how."

Mitch's remorse was so tangible, Jared shuddered. "Sometimes you can't fix what's broken, Mitch," he said. "Those are the things you have to let God fix."

Mitch dropped his gaze. "I've done some awful things, Jared. Can you find someone if…?"

Jared waited, but Mitch grew reflective. "Is there someone you want me to find?" Mitch trembled. What had Mitch done to cause such anguish in his soul? Fear tightened Jared's chest. He'd always been able to smooth things over for his stepbrother. What if this time he couldn't?

Mitch stared at the tent opening, then shook his head.

Jared sensed Mitch's frustration. "I'll reschedule my meeting and stay."

"No. Absolutely not. You go."

"You're more important to me than this meeting," Jared said.

"I know that and love you for it, bro. But I can do this on my own."

Jared hated leaving Mitch like this, but he was right. If he wasn't given a chance to test his new faith, he'd never grow. Jared picked up his jacket, then hesitated. "I'll try to wrap up my meeting fast and see you back here. You sure you'll be okay?"

Mitch nodded, then smiled, relaxing the worry lines along his mouth. "I'll be okay. Promise."

Apprehension gnawed at Jared's confidence, but he headed for the booth entrance, then turned. "One of the bull fighters I ran into gave me a piece of good advice. She said to not let fear defeat you. It's good advice, Mitch. Look it in the eye in your personal life and in the arena. And trust God for the rest."

Mitch slid into a chair and thumbed through Jared's worn Bible. "Say a prayer for me, Jared. I'm a little uneasy about tonight."

"You're in God's hands, Mitch. There's no better place to be."

Jared hurried out of the booth, anxious to conclude his business and return to the rodeo grounds. He was his brother's keeper and Mitch needed him. He should be here. The breath of a prayer whispered on his lips. He lifted his gaze and instantly collided with a clown-clad whirlwind.

The impact knocked the red and blue wig to the ground, loosening a pile of blond hair held up with pins. Soft brown lashes lifted to reveal eyes almost too big for such delicate features. Her feet tottered.

"Clarabelle." He clasped both of her arms firmly. Earlier, he'd been so wrapped up worrying about Mitch that he hadn't appreciated the woman's classical beauty now hidden behind clown's makeup. Her violet eyes locked with his, stealing his breath. "We meet again. Are you all right?"

A startled gasp escaped her over-painted mouth. She pulled away and stepped back. Picking up the wig, she clutched it between her fingers. "Clarabelle?" she said.

"Seemed appropriate for a lady clown. You're sure you're all right?"

"I'm fine. Did I hurt you?"

He took a deep breath, but his pulse continued to race. "No," he said, offering a smile.

Haley swallowed and stepped back, frightened by the strength in his hands and warmth in his eyes.

"Maybe I should try again," she said, hoping the bite in her voice would deter further interest.

She skirted around him and rushed off. Rounding the corner, she glanced back. He stood where she'd left him, staring after her with a puzzled, almost comical expression on his face. Haley broke contact and entered the arena through a side entrance, but the memory of his eyes stayed.

Someone touched her shoulder. She sucked in a breath and spun around, expecting to see the stranger, but Chester Rawlins, the other clown working the arena, grinned back.

"Girl, you're jumpier than a flea on a dog," he said.

"Nervous energy. I'll work it off."

"Hope so," he said, plopping a baseball cap on his head. "Rodeo's about to start. Let's go."

Tension heightened her anticipation. She reset the wig and purged the stranger from her mind. Her job began when the chute opened, not after the eight-second count.

The announcer introduced the first rider, and Haley waited. Every performance, she put her life on the line for these riders. She mustn't fail. She moved to the side as the first bull leaped from the gate, making short work of the rider. Haley drew the animal's attention while the cowboy dusted the dirt from his chaps and reached for his hat.

The next few hours passed in a blur. She and Chester worked the bulls like a valve and piston. She paused a moment to wipe her damp face, leaving a good portion of the face paint on the towel tucked into her suspenders. Resurrection's name blared over the speaker.

Haley choked back a cry. Fear swirled in the arena dust, settling at her feet, gnawing at her confidence. Sitting behind the barrier protecting the spectators, Hap nodded encouragement. She reset the rubber barrel and waited.

Resurrection stood quietly in the chute, submitting to his handlers as the rider checked the rigging and centered himself, his face hidden behind his hat brim. Haley knew the minute the gate opened the whole arena would be filled with two thousand pounds of raging fury bent on unseating and maiming the man, and her as well.

The cowboy nodded. The gate opened. Resurrection shot out of the chute. Haley kept the bull in her sights. The rider tossed like a doll and but kept his balance. Resurrection bellowed, arched his back and spun around, his leg buckling as he landed.

Haley held her breath as the man tipped sideways and fought to stay upright. The seconds seemed suspended, stretching her nerves to the snapping point. Resurrection ducked his head and twisted.

The buzzer sounded. Moving in front of the crazed bull, Haley and Chester tried to draw Resurrection's attention so the cowboy could dismount, but the bull ignored them and began a series of spins. He twisted hard right, then left.

The cowboy fell over the bull's side, his gloved hand trapped in the rigging. His legs bounced between the massive hooves. Haley's heart hammered against her chest. She reached for the rigging while Chester moved to the bull's other side. His rear hoof clipped Chester's leg. Haley caught a glimpse of two men helping him to the sidelines. She was on her own.

Resurrection's shoulder slammed into her, knocking her off balance. Her wig flew off, and her hair tumbled free. Something warm spurted onto her tongue. The familiar taste of fear rose in her throat. How had she ever thought she was a match for this animal?

Resurrection kicked sideways, catching the

cowboy's leg. His bone snapped, pulling a pained scream from his lips. Haley lunged forward, caught the rigging between her fingers and pulled. The man's pain-filled eyes connected with hers. A suffocating sensation tightened her throat. Sarah's eyes.

"You," she gasped. She yanked the rigging free and released him. The force knocked her to the ground. She rose in a daze. Resurrection circled the arena, challenging all efforts to herd him toward the exit.

The cowboy looked at her with eyes full of pain, then recognition, and something else she couldn't quite define.

"I'm sorry," he screamed. "I'm sorry."

Resurrection pawed the dirt. The wild look in his eyes held Haley immobile. The noise dimmed and the world seemed to move in slow motion, sending her back to a place she didn't want to be and time she didn't want to remember.

"Get him out of there, Haley," Chester yelled.

Haley closed her eyes, reliving in a flash the two incidents that had forever changed her life. Mitch and Resurrection. Two memories converged into one arena.

Resurrection charged. Two feet from her, he pivoted, catching Mitch between his horns and tossing him into the air. Mitch landed with a thud. The bull pounded his limp body.

Haley latched on to her shredded confidence. Ignoring her pain, she grabbed Resurrection's tail and yanked hard, then darted forward and smacked his shoulder. The bull spun around, pawed the ground and charged again. Haley moved in front of Mitch. Resurrection stopped, lifted his head and grunted, then pivoted and trotted out the gate. Mitch lay where he had fallen. Silence hung over the arena.

A new anguish seared her heart. The world spun around her, as though she was viewing someone else's life from a distance and not her own. Her knees buckled. Hap rushed through the gate and caught her before she hit the ground. Her whole body shook with a force that seemed to move the earth.

"I froze, Hap. I killed him. I killed Sarah's father."

Chapter Two

"**Y**ou're set to go," the nurse said, taking the release form from Haley. "Take it easy, now. You're going to be sore for a while."

Haley slid off the exam table and touched the bandage covering her stitches. Every muscle protested. She stood up and moved toward the door. A call button blinked in the next room. "If you have any problems, don't hesitate to come back," the nurse said, disappearing behind the next curtain.

Little by little, warmth seeped back into Haley's veins, bringing with it a wretchedness of mind she'd never known before. She glanced at the clock. Nearly nine-thirty. Barely an hour had passed since she'd agreed to let Hap bring her to the hospital and check her over. The emergency room was almost empty; the halls quiet, except for the steady blip of a monitor and the puff, hiss of the oxygen feed coming from a room down the hall. His room.

She had to pull herself together before facing Hap. The stitches in her forehead throbbed. Her body ached with reddening bruises. But bruises would heal. She wasn't so sure about her spirit.

She should leave and never look back, but the room drew her like an invisible magnet. Not the room. Him. He drew her. She'd put him here. In spite of everything, she couldn't walk away. What if he died? What if he lived? What would that mean for Sarah? If he found out about Sarah…

Her mouth moistened with bile. She inched down the hall and stopped at the glass partition, touching the scrawled name card beside the exam room. Mitch Jessup. She'd never thought about him as a person— until now. He'd been a monster in her nightmares. A name she'd chosen to forget—until now. Fear made her step back, but an unseen hand seemed to urge her forward. She stepped into the room.

Mitch's pale face blended into the pillowcase as though he was a part of it. Several bags hung from a pole, connected to him through IV tubes. The nurse pushed medication into one, then adjusted the fluid drip and looked up.

"Must have been some wreck," she said. "Are you a relative?"

Haley's hand shook. They *were* related. Through Sarah. "Sort of." She looked away. "How bad is he?"

"Stable for now. He's headed for surgery. The doctor's reviewing the X-rays. He'll be back," she said.

"I'll wait if you don't mind."

"It's good that he's not alone."

The nurse checked Mitch's pulse, gave Haley's arm a pat and left. Haley edged closer. A deep gash ran along his jaw. Cuts streaked his arms, some stitched, some held together by butterfly strips. She suspected the worst injuries lay hidden beneath the sheet. His dark hair stood out against the pillow. Sunken cheeks gave his face a death-like appearance. Except for the shallow rise and fall of his chest, he looked like a corpse, nothing like the man she'd met at the carnival that hot July night eight years ago.

She'd lied to Pop about where she was going, knowing full well he would refuse to let her go. She'd seen the tall, handsome cowboy the moment she'd entered the gate—felt his eyes roam over her. He had a strong square jaw with full, high cheekbones; crisp dark hair that curled around his neck and a dazzling smile that made her heart skip.

He was older, worldly and smooth, and just a tad drunk. But not so drunk that he hadn't known what he was doing. He was all the forbidden things she'd been told to stay away from and everything that enticed an innocent teen full of curiosity and whimsical dreams.

"I'm Haley," she'd offered.

His grin had turned her knees to Jell-O. "Hello, Haley." He bowed. "Mitch Jessup, at your service. But you can call me Lancelot. Seems my Guinevere has stood me up."

"I'll be Gwen," she'd murmured.

He'd touched her arm. "I'd like that. Wanna ride the carousel with me?" He'd leaned toward her, his lips only inches from hers. The flirtation seemed so trivial then. Not so, now.

The monitor blipped again. Haley jumped, stepped back, then moved closer to the bed, blocking her thoughts, holding the past behind the barrier that had preserved her for so long.

She wanted him to suffer, not die. If he died, it would be on her head, one more guilt to add to her list of sins. A sob escaped her lips. She closed her eyes and squeezed her head between her hands, unwilling to face him, unable to turn away.

"Haley," Mitch whispered. "It is you."

She opened her eyes and backed toward the door. Reason told her he couldn't hurt her. He was too busted up. But fear didn't know reason. He lifted his arm and groaned.

"Don't go."

Haley's legs shook, but she stopped inching toward the door. "I've hated you for so long." Her gaze drifted over him, avoiding his eyes. "I never wanted this."

His eyes glazed with pain. "I know. Not your fault. None of it...."

Tears welled in her eyes. "You took everything," she said. "My trust, my innocence. All you left in me was shame and fear."

His eyes closed. "I'm sorry."

"Sorry...isn't...enough. I want you to hurt, like you've hurt me."

His head moved back and forth as though her words haunted him. "If I could…change that night… God knows."

Haley clenched her teeth. "Don't you dare drop the God bomb on me."

Mitch's attempted smile ended in a grimace. "Felt that way once or twice." His body spasmed. He caught his breath. "God can heal this. Heal us."

"Us…?" She shrank from the word, from his pleading eyes. "I'll never forgive you for what you did."

"No." He looked incredibly tired. "Forgive yourself." He gasped and looked straight through her. "Give God the hurt. Only way past it." He gasped, then closed his gray-green eyes.

Sarah's eyes.

Haley's breath caught. Whatever else Mitch Jessup was, he was Sarah's father. Something inside her knotted like tangled rope.

Mitch's lips quivered. "Don't let what I did…keep you in darkness."

His chin dipped a tad, rose as though he were struggling to remain awake, then his head rolled sideways. Haley took a step forward and stopped.

Don't you dare die.

For a brief moment his chest stilled, then moved. She released her breath with the movement. Sorry wasn't enough to make up for what he'd destroyed. Mitch Jessup planted her child with violence. She wanted him to pay, not die.

Don't live in darkness. Let God have it.

Anger burned through her. God had abandoned her behind a vacant booth that night, holding a basket full of destroyed dreams. God had left her nurturing a life she hadn't asked for and wouldn't destroy.

The wounds God had allowed denied her all that she dreamed of, leaving her fearful of intimacy, unable to shed the shackles of the past, unable to give Sarah or herself the kind of life they wanted.

And now God had allowed this man back into her life. To what purpose? If God had forgiven Mitch Jessup after what he'd done, she wanted no part of God. There was no way she could ever forgive Mitch.

"Forgive me," he pleaded.

She shook her head. "I can't."

"I'm sorry." Anguish rang in his whispered words.

Haley hardened her heart. "It isn't enough."

She pivoted and rushed down the hall, away from his pleading eyes and wasting body. Someone called to her, but she didn't answer. She shoved the emergency door open and gulped in a cleansing breath, but the tepid air couldn't erase the smell of death any more than the night's darkness could hide what her mind held.

Hap's battered truck waited by the curb, empty. She yanked the door open and slid inside, resting her head against the worn upholstery. A few minutes later, he slid into the seat beside her.

"Somebody light yer tail on fire?" he said softly.

Haley jerked upright. Pain shot through her neck and sides. She wanted to leave this place and all of its memories behind and never look back. But now and forever, they would follow. Sarah was all that mattered. She must protect Sarah.

"Where were you?" she asked.

Hap handed her a steaming cup of coffee. "Looking for you. Didn't you hear me call to you? Ya scared that nice nurse right outta her shoes takin' off like that."

Haley took a big gulp, scalding her tongue, welcoming the pain that drew her back from the past. "I didn't see her."

Hap slanted a look her way and started the engine. His gray eyes filled with sympathy. "Saw the doc. He said you're going to be sore but okay. Not so sure about the other fella." Hap pulled out of the parking lot. "Thought about what you plan to tell Sarah?"

Haley glanced back at the hospital entrance. "That I'm battered but okay."

Hap eased into a turn with the same quiet manner he did everything. Even in the darkness, she could almost picture the well-oiled wheels in his mind rewinding the video, viewing and analyzing each event in detail. A street light illuminated his face. He glanced her way. In a flash she saw his hurt, not for himself, but for her and Sarah. Tears stung her eyes.

"You don't have to shade the facts no more. Your Pop ain't here for you to protect, Haley. Even if he was, he'd understand. Do you plan to tell Sarah the truth about her father?" he asked without reproof or absolution.

"The truth, Hap? What is the truth?"

He turned the truck again, bringing the fair-grounds into view. "Wasn't sure until I saw you leaving that young man's room. Things never did set right with your story. Didn't happen the way you said, did it?" He reached a hand out and patted her arm. "What do you plan to do about it?"

His face turned toward her, his compassion covered by darkness. Haley's pulse hammered against her throat.

"Nothing. I can't, Hap. And for Sarah's sake, you won't either."

Jared raced into Mitch's room as the nurse injected something into Mitch's IV and unlocked the bed wheels. Tubes and needles poked from Mitch's body. Jared slid to a stop, too stunned to move.

"Jared?" the nurse asked, rolling Mitch's bed toward the elevator.

"Yes."

"He's been asking for you. You can go part of the way to surgery with us."

"How bad?" Jared said.

The nurse poked the elevator button, but didn't look up. "I've seen worse," she said, checking the IV flow.

Jared took Mitch's hand and felt a weak squeeze. "I'm here, Mitch. I understand you rode Resurrection."

"Yeah." Mitch's voice faded. "Rode him. Bull still won. You should've seen it."

"Guess that means you'll have to retire for a while on your winnings until you get better."

Mitch's hand went slack. Jared held on as the elevator ascended to the second floor.

"Won't get…better. Your meeting…" Mitch whispered.

"Went well," Jared said, shutting out the fear gnawing at his throat. "I should have been here."

Mitch's heavy lids opened, revealing eyes that seemed to see into another dimension. "We didn't know my ride would be rescheduled. God did. As it should be…" His voice faded. "Where is she?"

Jared glanced at the nurse. "Who?"

Mitch gulped in a breath. "Haley. She was here."

"There was a young woman here earlier but I think she left," the nurse explained. "She said she was family."

"Who's Haley, Mitch?" Jared asked.

Mitch struggled to stay awake. "I…. Don't let her go…" He swallowed. "I…need to forgive…"

The words slurred together, not making sense. Jared bent closer. The connection with Mitch faded.

"You hang on, Mitch." Jared gripped the bed rail. "You hear me? Hang on. I need you."

"Promise," Mitch said.

"Anything. What?"

Mitch's fingers circled Jared's hand. "Haley gets the money." His eyes closed. "I'm so sorry. So sorry."

The elevator doors opened. A male attendant scrambled in to assist the nurse. Jared trotted to keep up as they pulled the gurney toward the surgery's double doors.

"Wait here," the attendant said. "Someone will check in with you later."

Jared's heart pounded against his chest.

Mitch's lips parted. "It's okay. I'm ready to go. Remember…promise."

Jared's gut clamped. "I'll remember, Mitch. But you're going to be all right."

The doors banged shut, cutting off Jared's words. He winced and stared through the glass until Mitch disappeared behind another set of doors. The hall was quiet, dark and empty. He stuffed his hands into his pockets and headed back to the waiting room.

Memories burned his mind—high school rodeos, football games, prom. Their parents had married when Jared was in the fifth grade and Mitch a year behind. Every important event in their lives had been shared. He raked a hand through his hair and glanced around the room. Empty paper cups and wadded tissues lay scattered in the waiting room, remnants from the last occupants. A hardback Bible sat isolated on a table.

Jared sank into the chair and ran his fingers over the gold lettering. For eight years Mitch had been out of his reach. He'd searched and prayed, desperate to keep Mitch out of trouble, but Jared hadn't been able to protect him. He couldn't protect him now. He squeezed the Bible between his hands. He couldn't lose his brother. Mitch had to live.

Jared bowed his head. *Please, God, don't let Mitch die.*

He passed the hours pleading to God on Mitch's behalf. Then the hospital paging system crackled.

"Code blue."

Chapter Three

Six days later, Jared parked behind the Fellowship Booth and headed down the midway. The memory of Walt Jessup's crumpled form at Mitch's gravesite was too raw to revisit. He'd do anything to ease his stepfather's pain. Focusing on the truth about Mitch's accident was a welcome diversion. He'd reviewed the playback tapes and asked Sam McIntosh, the association president, for an investigation, hoping what he believed he'd seen on the tapes was wrong. He paused beside an empty booth and watched the milling people.

"Clarabelle," he murmured to himself. The violet-eyed clown he'd spoken to the day Mitch died formed clearly in his mind. Clarabelle and Mitch's Haley were one and the same. An odd feeling of disappointment punched his gut. "Who are you?" he whispered. "And why would Mitch leave you his winnings without telling his family anything about you?"

He shut out the loud music and joined the flow of people. He'd frozen the replay tape from the moment where it seemed Mitch had recognized Haley, then played the rest in slow motion, right up to the moment Mitch lay still in the dirt. The more he watched the replay, the more he felt the tangible connection between the bullfighter and his brother. It was as though for a split second, the screen had come alive.

Something wasn't right. When he'd seen Haley near the bull pens, she'd spoken of facing fear. He'd seen her fear on the replay. Had her fear caused Mitch's death? If so, he couldn't let it go. Mitch deserved justice. Jared needed answers, and he was certain Haley had them.

He pictured her face again. His fingers and nose tingled as he remembered her soft skin beneath his steadying grasp and the fresh scent of the soap lingering on her flesh. He tensed, the memory surprising him.

The midway sparkled in the afternoon sun. Laughter and music filled the air. The sun half-hid behind a cluster of clouds, forming a halo of bright light with descending rays that seemed to touch the earth—almost as though the heavens rejoiced in catching Mitch's spirit and carrying it up to God.

God, Mitch made his peace with You. Help me make peace with his death.

He waited for God's peace to ease the pain. But nothing came. Only an emptiness left by Mitch's passing and lots of unanswered questions. The arena speaker hummed, announcing the line-up for barrel competitions. He shifted direction and weaved through the crowd toward the horse corrals. The announcer's voice echoed between the stands.

"Next up, in third place, a circuit favorite, Haley Clayton, on Spinner…"

Jared drew a sharp breath and edged along the fence toward the gate. A dun horse shot through the opening. The woman's face passed in a blur. Horse and rider moved in unison, cleared the first barrel and raced toward the second.

Jared glanced at the clock as the pair formed a cloverleaf around the second barrel. The big gelding tightened the circle around the third, but the woman's toe clipped the barrel edge, tipping it into the dirt. That mistake would knock her out of the big money. She ducked her head, leaned low across the horse's back and raced for the gate.

Jared slipped around the steel panel into the paddock area. If Mitch's death had affected her performance, it certainly hadn't pricked her enough to attend his funeral or send condolences.

Haley dismounted and stood beside the fence, her slender shoulders stooped in disappointment while her fingers stroked the white star on the gelding's forehead. A long braid hung down her back. The gold-fringe on her red shirt matched her hair. A narrow, silver-studded belt emphasized her small waist.

"Haley," he said, stopping behind her.

She turned and tipped her hat back. A pair of vivid

violet eyes rounded with recognition. Her left eyebrow lifted a fraction. A tremor touched her smooth lips. Her skin glowed with a beauty previously hidden behind clown makeup. A yellowing bruise discolored her cheek. Bangs partially concealed a flesh-colored bandage on her forehead. She half-turned and flipped the stirrup over the horse's back, then loosened the latigo holding the cinch in place.

"We meet again," he said.

A shadow passed over her face and quickly disappeared. "Are you following me?" she asked.

"No," he said, moving toward the horse's head. "I'm Jared Sinclair, Mitch Jessup's brother."

Her eyes flattened and went cold. Her fingers curled around the buckle like a lifeline. She stepped back, catching her spurs in the dirt. Jared reached for her elbow but she pulled away. "I'd like to talk to you about what happened the night Mitch died."

She focused her gaze on his boots. "I'm sorry your brother died, but I don't see how going over it will help you. It won't change what happened."

"Maybe not. But I still need to hear it from someone who was close to him."

"We weren't close." Haley lifted her head, her beautiful eyes focusing on his chin. Wariness darkened them, turning them almost purple.

"I meant close by," Jared said. Suspicion nudged his mind.

"Lots of people were there. Why don't you talk to them?"

Mitch's voice rang through Jared's mind. *Don't let her go…forgive.*

"I want to talk to *you*. Mitch asked me to find you," Jared said. If Haley was responsible for Mitch's death, there was no way he was going to just let her walk away from it like nothing had happened. "I'd like to know why," he said.

Her face paled. "I can't imagine why."

"I think you do."

She caught her breath, then shifted the reins back and forth in her hands.

Jared felt her fear, sensed deception at work, but if he wanted answers, truthful answers, he'd have to use softer tactics. "Please, Haley. I just need to know what happened to my brother."

Doubt flickered across her face. She dropped her gaze. "I can tell you what I remember. Everything happened so fast, some details are jumbled," she murmured.

She seemed to choose her words carefully. Jared moved to the horse's side, forcing her to look right at him.

"Try. I want to know everything that happened between the time Mitch entered the arena and the time he was carried out. And I want to hear it from you."

Her gaze shifted toward the exit. She buried her fingers in the gelding's mane and combed through the thick hairs. For someone who had nothing to hide, she was acting guilty about something. Disappointment centered in Jared's chest. The sights and sounds dimmed until it seemed the only ones occupying this space were he and Haley—and the mystery surrounding her and Mitch.

"There isn't much to tell," she said. "His ride was normal until the dismount. His hand got caught in the rigging. I pulled it free and we got knocked in the dirt. The impact shook us both." She fidgeted, letting silence fall between them. Her voice caught, then lowered. "Resurrection got to him before I did."

There was more in what she didn't say, in the way her eyes refused to meet his, the way her voice trembled with something more than just sorrow or regret. Mitch deserved to be heard and Jared intended to see this through, no matter how painful it proved to be.

"You knew this bull," he said. "You knew how dangerous he was. That's why you were at the pens that day."

She nodded. Her gaze swept the ground, then glazed as though her thoughts had taken a different direction. "I knew him. He's dangerous." She murmured so low he barely heard and was uncertain if she was referring to Mitch or the bull.

"You knew Mitch, too, didn't you, Haley?"

Her head snapped up. "No."

"You were with him at the hospital."

"I was there anyway." She touched the bandage on her forehead.

"Why didn't you stay?"

"I couldn't."

"Why?" he probed.

"I just couldn't. Why should I?"

"Did he say anything to you?"

Haley flinched. Fear widened her eyes, touching him in a way that made him regret his harshness but heightened his need for the truth.

The question snaked between them like a whip and struck her. She remembered only too well Mitch's last words. Words that still echoed in her head.

Forgive yourself.

How dare he tell her to forgive herself after what he'd done. She shook the memory loose.

"I think maybe he thought I was someone else."

"He didn't. He was very certain about your name and about wanting me to find you." Jared's brown eyes probed hers.

"I have to go," she said. "If you're looking to blame someone, I can't help you. I did what I could and I'm truly sorry."

"Sorry? Sorry that he died or that your moment of fear may have caused his death?"

Jared's square jaw clenched, giving his rugged face a determined, hard look. Haley's stomach roiled. He was too close to the truth for comfort. If he found out about Sarah, what would happen then? Panic rose to her throat. He emitted the same power she'd sensed the first time she'd run into him outside the bull pens six days ago. How much like Mitch was Jared? *Don't make an enemy of this man,* she cautioned herself.

She finished loosening the cinch, aware that he

watched, gauged and absorbed every move. The sun dipped toward the distant mountains. Haley shivered in spite of the heat. She mustn't give him cause to pursue his questions.

Jared's glance sharpened. "How well did you know my brother, Haley?"

She lifted her chin, forcing herself to stare into his eyes. She would not cower before this man or any other. And she wouldn't own Mitch's sins. Heaven knew she had enough of her own to atone for.

"I told you I didn't *know* him. We met briefly several years ago. I didn't see him again until the night he rode Resurrection."

"But you *had* met him before so why did you deny it? You told the nurse at the hospital you were family."

"Meeting doesn't constitute knowing. I was in that arena with him. Two years ago I was laying in the same spot that he was. I needed to know and the doctors wouldn't tell me anything." She shrugged.

"Then why not just say so?" Silence hung between them like dust in an arena.

Her heart dropped. Caught in the deception. She glanced at her watch and moved around Spinner. "I don't know.

"I watched the replays."

Her fist clenched in the animal's mane. "Is there a point to all this? You weren't in there. You don't know. I have to go."

Jared stepped aside. His hand, large and rough, touched her wrist. She shivered again.

"Don't go far, Haley," he said. "There's more to this than what you've told me. I can find truth in the most unlikely places. You and I are not through."

Haley tugged on Spinner's reins and rushed from the paddock without looking back. Jared had her so confused she didn't know which way was up. Behind the barns, she bent over, rested her hands on her knees, and gulped in waves of fresh air, but it didn't stem the nausea rising to her throat. Spinner nuzzled her neck and nickered.

She led the horse into the barn. When she chanced a look behind her there was no sign of Jared, but she could still feel his power, the air of authority surrounding him, the tingle along her skin that remained long after she'd pulled away from him.

He'd thrown down an invisible gauntlet, and instinct told her he would stop at nothing to discover the truth.

The sun dropped behind the horizon, painting the sky a dark orange. Hap plugged the horse trailer lights into his truck and rechecked the hitch and safety chains, while Haley hooked the camper to her truck.

"Never known you to run from nothing," he said.

Haley placed a finger to her lips and watched Sarah stuff a horse blanket into Hap's truck cab. If she and Sarah could get safely back to Hap's place, Jared would have a hard time finding them.

"There's no reason to stay when there's work waiting at home."

"It's not fair," Sarah said, sticking her lips out.

"Why don't you go? Hap and I can come later. After the finals. We never miss the finals."

"We'll go together," Haley said.

Sarah's eyes watered in frustration. "Can I go and at least say goodbye to my friends?"

Haley's heart thudded like a trapped rabbit. "Go. But stay in sight of the truck. I don't want to have to come looking for you. You've got ten minutes."

Hap's silent disapproval cut into the evening air louder than the music coming from the midway. She never should have told him everything.

"Runnin' stinks, don't it?" he said.

Haley moved toward her own truck, which seemed to groan beneath the weight of the camper. "I'm protecting Sarah."

"He's her family, too."

"How do I know he's any different than Mitch?"

"You don't."

Haley locked the camper door and leaned her head against the cool metal. "Don't, Hap. Don't take his side. What if he finds out about Sarah?"

Hap patted her arm, then squeezed her shoulder.

"Sarah's mine. She can't know where she came from. She's too young." Haley turned and leaned against him.

"You didn't do nothin' wrong, girl. You can't run from this."

Haley's eyes misted. "Sarah doesn't need any family but you and me."

"Maybe God thinks otherwise."

"Don't," she said.

Hap's rough hand stroked her hair. "Ain't you forgettin'? Sarah's God's child. There's a reason He placed her with you—a reason He allowed her to come into this world the way she did. And there's a reason this man is here now."

Haley spun around, grabbed the camper jack and rammed it into the truck bed. "Well, I wish God would enlighten me."

"Maybe you ain't listenin'. Wouldn't be the first time," he said.

Haley jammed her hat onto her head. "I suppose you're going to tell me too that God had a reason for Mitch being here and a reason that I...played a part in killing him." She brushed away a tear.

"You didn't kill nobody."

"If it had been any other cowboy…"

"What's written is written, honey. And God holds the pen that does the writin'."

She kicked a rock and sent it flying across the parking lot. "I don't want him poking around."

Hap stroked his chin. "Secrets won't stay hidden forever."

Haley caught Sarah's glance, the rebellious look still in her eyes.

Hap motioned Sarah to wait. "Face the man now. Don't wait for him to come to you."

"Tell him what his brother was and seal our fate? Not a chance."

Hap raked a hand through his silver hair and

sighed. "Stay and finish this. I'll take Sarah home with me and you won't need to mention her at all."

Haley rubbed her arms, feeling a chill in the warm air.

"You need to make him see that you *are* sorry the boy died." Hap pinned her with his gaze. "You are sorry, aren't you?"

"You know I am."

"He needs to that." Hap tipped his hat back.

"I *do* feel responsible, Hap. Responsible and…relieved. It was an accident, but with Mitch gone, I thought that now it was finally over. I could put an end to all those bad dreams. What does that say about me?"

"That you're human and that you can't do this alone." Hap scuffed his toe in the dust. "Haley, you gotta let God help with this."

Haley glanced at Sarah and swallowed the knot in her throat. Hap could very well be right. But trusting didn't come easy. Especially where God was concerned. She wasn't sure it ever would. "I can't. But I will stay. I'll finish this."

Hap gave a satisfied nod and loaded the horses in his trailer. "I'll get the rest of the stuff from the barn," he said.

The memory of Jared's dark eyes filled her mind, how their warmth the day he'd bumped in to her outside the Fellowship tent had both touched and frightened her, how they'd gleamed like hard shards of rock when he'd questioned her about the accident and knowing Mitch.

She'd backed herself into a corner, and he knew it. If he pushed her too far, he wouldn't like what she had to say. She rechecked the hitch and chains on the camper and fished in her pocket for the keys. Footsteps crunched the gravel behind her.

"I'm almost ready, Hap."

She turned around and stared straight into Jared's flashing dark eyes.

"Going somewhere?" he asked.

She searched frantically for Hap, then saw Sarah wave to her friends and skip toward her.

Chapter Four

Jared watched the child approach. Her movements smacked with familiarity, rekindling old memories of another time and place, memories of a young boy with unruly jet-black hair tagging along behind him with the same bounce in his step and tilt to his head. The puzzle pieces were starting to come together. The first shock wave knocked him like a mule's kick.

Every movement right down to her furrowed brow bore traces of the brother he'd lost. Her black hair refused to be tamed by braids and streamed in a tangled mass around her face. She lifted her chin and darted a look at him. Another shock wave ripped through Jared, pain so intense it stole his breath.

"Hi. I'm Sarah," she said holding his gaze with gray-green eyes.

Jared opened his mouth but nothing came out. This child was a feminine replica of Mitch. She had to be Mitch's daughter. Obviously Haley hadn't expected to see Mitch again. That was the reason he'd seen recognition and shock on the replay tapes, the reason her answers were less than satisfactory. Sarah was the secret Haley was hiding, the secret that may have cost Mitch his life.

The color drained from Haley's face. Like a bear protecting her young, she moved between him and Sarah. "Sarah Rose. Go to the barn and find Hap," she said.

"But, Mom—"

"Go. Now."

Sarah bounced an uncertain look between them and raced toward the barn. Jared watched until she was out of sight. He wanted to reach out and touch her, make sure she was real. She was so like Mitch it made him ache. Haley had kept Sarah from Mitch, from Walt, from all of them. Why? Anger waged a tug of war inside him.

"She's Mitch's daughter, isn't she, Haley? Did he know?" The question nearly choked him. "What really happened in the arena the night Mitch died?"

He heard the steel in his own voice. She winced, then grabbed his arm and pulled him away from the truck, away from the barns and from Sarah. "She's *my* daughter. Go away. You have no right to hound me."

"Mitch's death gives me that right," he said looking toward the barn. Jared shook with rage. Only God would be able to help her if he was right. "Look me in the eye and tell me that child isn't his and that you didn't deliberately keep her from him. From her grandparents."

She couldn't. She knew it and so did he. "Sarah has a right to know her family," he said. "We just lost Mitch, and Sarah is a living part of him. We have a right to know her." His chest tightened. He fisted his hands against his sides.

Haley flattened herself against the truck. "You have no rights and neither did Mitch. He lost that the second he left me behind that—"

She covered her mouth with her hand. She wouldn't—couldn't—think about that night or speak of it ever. Not with this man or any other. The fury in Jared's eyes terrified her. The realization of what he wanted, expected, was unthinkable.

She looked toward the barn and saw Sarah pulling Hap toward them, his bum leg sliding in the dirt, kicking dust into the evening air. "I can't talk to you about this now."

He followed her gaze. His eyes narrowed when they rested on Sarah, then softened. For a moment she thought he would refuse, that he would lie in wait, snatch Sarah away and disappear. A hand clenched around her soul.

"When?" he said.

"Tomorrow. I'll meet you at the bull pens in the morning."

His gaze shifted back to her and hardened. "Be there, Haley. If you run, I'll find you."

He spun around without looking back and disappeared into the crowd, his threat hanging in the air like heavy fog. Haley's whole body shook. She gripped the truck and gulped in a breath, felt Hap and Sarah's presence behind her, then Hap's hand touched her shoulder and Sarah's small fingers closed around hers.

"Mom? Are you okay? Who was that man?"

The endless night finally broke, sending a streak of red across the horizon. Haley headed toward the bull pens taking comfort in the familiar surroundings. Meeting Jared felt safer with Hap and Sarah out of Wyoming and back in Colorado, even if she hadn't answered Sarah's questions to satisfaction. One more strike against Jared Sinclair.

The sounds and smells around the stock pens rose in the morning air. Haley slowed her step, then stopped. Jared stood in front of Resurrection's pen, his profile outlined beneath a wide-brimmed hat. His arms were draped over the top rail, his eyes locked on the bull. She wondered if he, too, had been avoiding Resurrection's pen. Even from a distance, she saw his chin tighten, then his hand brushed over his face.

Her heart squeezed. He was an enemy, a threat to herself and Sarah. She couldn't see him as a man grieving a loss, but she couldn't ignore it either.

"I'm here," she said.

Jared lifted his head, turned and faced her. Shadows lingered beneath his eyes. He hadn't shaved and the stubble darkening his face made him forbidding. She took a backward step.

"I should have been here," Jared said.

His pain mingled with her own. Haley ignored the warning buzzing in her head. "It wouldn't have mattered," she said. "There are no rules with Resurrection. You couldn't have stopped what happened." She hesitated a moment, then added, "Neither could I."

"We'll never know for certain," he said pulling his jacket collar up. "But that's not why we're here, is it? You see, Haley, it's not the beginning or the end that matters most now. It's the space in between."

The space that included Sarah. The beginning did matter, to her, but he loved his brother. Sympathy vanished in a rush of white-hot anger. "Don't presume you know me or anything about me."

His gaze traveled her face, then locked on her eyes. Haley wished she could crawl inside his head and know what he was thinking. This guessing was like falling off a cliff in slow motion.

"That's the whole point. None of us really *know* anything, do we? I'll make this clear and direct. Sarah has a grandfather who feels he's lost everything. The truth is, he hasn't." Tense silence stretched between them. "Mitch isn't here to speak for himself, so I'll do it for him. He deserves justice for what you kept from him. I want you and Sarah to come to South Dakota to meet…"

Haley gasped, certain Resurrection had gut kicked her, but the animal stood quietly, his nose buried in a mound of alfalfa. Her legs threatened to buckle. She shook her head.

Jared lifted a brow. "Is that a no?" he said in a harsh, raw voice.

She looked up, forcing herself to meet his gaze without flinching. "That's a never."

"Mitch made bad choices for a lot of years," Jared said. "In the last few months, he'd turned his life around. He was pulling things together. Trying to right the wrongs."

"And for that he deserves…what?"

His eyes flashed. Haley moved to the corral and stared at Resurrection. Jared moved beside her. "After I left you last night, I thought a lot about everything that's happened. Mitch walked away from you and Sarah. Away from his responsibilities. I get that. I think I understand some things that I didn't before."

Haley's hand fisted. "You understand nothing!" She raised her fist to strike him. He caught her hand, his grip around her wrist powerful and painful. She trembled but stared him down.

If he wanted the truth, she could stomp him into the dust with it. But she couldn't revisit a place that had taken her years to get past. His grip tightened. She struggled, kicking at his legs.

"Haley. Stop it."

He released her. She stepped back. Several people were staring at them. She turned away and gripped the corral panels with shaking hands. The wound that had never really healed ripped open.

"Sometimes people aren't what you think they are," she said. "Sometimes by the time you figure that out, the chute's already opened and it's too late to change the ride. Don't do this." He didn't touch her again, but she felt his hold, like a noose around her neck.

"This isn't negotiable, Haley. You can tell your daughter about her father or leave it to a court. Bottom line is she has more family than just you." He pulled a pen and paper from his pocket and jotted down a number. "It's time to make things right," he said, his tone softening. "If I don't hear from you in three days, I'll come to Colorado and get you."

Haley's throat closed. "You wouldn't."

Jared took her hand and crammed the paper into her palm. "Three days. Call me."

Four hours later Haley pulled into the gravel lane leading to Hap's ranch. She backed the truck and camper under the old pole barn, shut off the engine and leaned back. Gray weathered boards with peeling white paint covered the old house. The outbuildings were ancient and in need of repair, but it was home. The only real home she'd ever known. Her throat tightened. She opened the door and slid from the seat. Across the barnyard, a door slammed. Gravel crunched beneath running feet. Sarah slid to a stop beside the truck, then threw her arms around Haley's waist.

"You're back. I'm sorry I was mad at you last night. Hap said you had to take care of a grown-up thing."

Haley looked into Sarah's gray-green eyes. The innocence and resiliency of her own childhood seemed like a distant memory but one she needed to preserve in Sarah.

How much she had lost. But how much she had gained.

"Hap's in the barn. Annie had her puppies last night. He said he needed to talk to you as soon as you got home."

"Then I'll go see him."

Sarah headed for the house. Haley crossed the barnyard and pulled the barn door open. Bales of fresh hay filled the usually musty barn with a fresh, clean scent.

Hap rose, lifting two squirmy mounds of black and white in his gnarled hands. "Born last night, just after we got home," he said. "Nice pups. Should bring a good price." He set the pups down and avoided looking at her. "Sam McIntosh called."

Air whooshed from Haley's lungs. "Sam?" She managed to choke out the association president's name. "What did he want?"

"Seems someone has requested an inquiry into Mitch's accident. Sam thought you should know."

Someone. Jared.

Haley's legs wobbled. She slid onto a bale and stared at the ground.

"You're on leave until the official inquiry is closed," Hap said quietly.

Suspended. Her livelihood and hard-earned reputation hung in the balance, dangling from a hangman's noose. And she knew who held the rope.

"Sam said it's just a formality and he was sure the ruling would be in your favor. Guess I don't need to ask how your meeting with Sinclair went."

Three days passed like a year. Every day Haley watched the road, waiting for Jared to make good on his promise. He was never far from her thoughts, and she hated the way he'd taken root in her mind, and stolen her sense of security and peace. She sent Sarah into town with Hap, knowing full well it would incur Jared's anger if he arrived and she wasn't there, but if he thought she would lie down and play dead so he could issue ultimatums and walk all over her, he could think again.

She drew Annie's pup close to her face, relishing the softness of newborn puppy. Tiny claws flailed against her cheek. The black nose scrunched, then a wet tongue latched around her nose and suckled. The scent of puppy breath lingered on her skin, fresh and new, helpless and innocent. Innocent. The word seemed to taunt her.

Mourning doves cooed in the barn rafters. Haley lifted her head and watched the sun slant through the weathered boards. This place had once been her refuge. As a child she used to come here and pour her heart out to God, just as Sarah sometimes did now. She had faith then. It all seemed like another lifetime.

If she sought God's help again, would He hear or turn a deaf ear to her plea like that night so long ago?

"Lord God." The desperate call brought tears to her eyes, remembrances of a time when her faith had been strong floated through her mind. "I haven't asked You for anything for a long time. Please hear me. I love my daughter. Don't take her from me," she murmured.

She sensed someone watching her, twisted around and caught her breath. Jared stood in the doorway, his hair glistening in the morning sun. So this was the answer to her prayer. She set her jaw, but her heart did a treacherous lurch. He was more attractive than she remembered, but that was his only saving grace. His heart was as black as his shadow.

"Do you always make a habit of sneaking up on people?" she asked, placing the pup at Annie's side.

"Only the ones I think might do something foolish, like run away," he said, watching her. "You didn't call. There wasn't anyone at the house and I'm a little surprised that I found you here."

"Sarah's at a birthday party. And where would I go? You made it clear that you'd hunt me to the ends of the earth."

He smiled, transforming harshness to handsome. "So you got the message."

"I got it. You've managed to steal my income and taint my reputation, so tell me, Mr. Sinclair, where would I go and what would I use to go with?"

A hint of compassion glistened in his eyes, angering her.

"You aren't fired, Haley, just sidelined for a while. I want the truth. I want justice. The investigation is my assurance that you won't disappear."

She lifted her chin. "I'm sorry Mitch died. Whatever our differences, I never wanted that to happen." She rose and moved around him, giving her easier access to the door. Her chest pounded, spreading fear through every pore in her body. "Does it make you feel better to sideline me without pay?"

Jared detected no pretense in her voice. Watching her with the pup, he'd caught a glimpse of another dimension to this woman. She was beautiful, but he sensed more depth to her than the women he knew Mitch usually associated with. This one stirred his curiosity.

"No, Haley. I'm not happy about this investigation, but I have to do it—for Mitch. And that brings me to the other reason I'm here."

"There's more than locking us in your trunk and whisking us away?"

Jared ground his teeth, but held his temper. He wasn't at all sure what he was about to do was right or ethical, but the request was the last thing he'd promised Mitch and no matter how much it galled him, he'd see it through.

"Mitch requested that you received the bounty money from his ride," Jared said, gauging her reaction.

Her eyes sparked. "Payment for services rendered? Blood money to salve a deathbed conscience," she said. Pink stained her cheeks. "I don't want it. Find some other cause to donate it to." Her voice simmered with bitterness.

"This $30,000 cost Mitch his life. If you don't want it, think of Sarah." Jared's misgivings increased by the minute. He had no doubt she meant every word. Still, her reactions ran deep enough to justify an act of revenge. A woman scorned thing. He didn't want to wrap his mind completely around that, but he'd promised Mitch, and that promise must be kept, no matter what. The weight of the investigation settled on his shoulders.

"Look at me, Haley."

Her violet gaze touched him. Her hands twisted nervously. Something flickered far back in her eyes. Jared's chest squeezed. She was afraid of him. The realization left him with a feeling of emptiness. She looked away. The clip holding her hair caught a flash of sun, sending rainbow prisms dancing across the ground, then in a flash of color, they splashed across his shirt.

Their tiny points seemed to stab into his chest. He wanted to know about her—her hopes, dreams, ambitions. Most of all, he wanted the truth and for the first time, dreaded the consequences it might bring. Justice belonged with God. Why couldn't he leave it there?

She whirled around and stepped into the sunlight. Jared followed, pulling an envelope from his pocket.

"This is a cashier's check made out to you." He held it out.

"You have no idea what you're asking me to do."

"Take it, Haley."

She stared at the envelope, then back at him. She took it, holding it away from her as though it were contaminated.

"How soon can you and Sarah be ready to go?" he asked.

Her gaze flew to his face. "Go?"

"I already told you that Sarah meeting Mitch's father wasn't an option."

Haley wadded the envelope in her fist. "She doesn't know about this."

"You've had three days."

"I tried. I just couldn't tell her." The air between them sizzled.

"Three days isn't nearly enough time to explain the last eight years." She lifted her chin. "I won't expose her to Mitch's family."

"Expose her?" Jared swallowed his anger, hating this fine line between righting Mitch's wrong and delivering justice for his brother's death. "You act like we're all a bunch of ax murders or something."

"That would be better than the truth," she murmured.

Jared raked a hand through his hair. "And what is the truth according to Haley? You and Mitch had a relationship that went bad, but you haven't given his family a chance. We just want a chance to know Mitch's daughter. We would never hurt you. I would never hurt you."

Shadows deepened under her eyes. Her face

closed, as if guarding a secret. "You already have. How can you ask me to trust that the son isn't like the father?" Her voice broke.

Jared noted eyes filled with sorrow, pain and fear. He saw it, felt it, and it tugged at something inside him. If Mitch used her and dumped her, turning her life upside down, how did he expect her to feel? She hadn't been given any reason to think his family was any different. And he hadn't helped. He'd pushed her into a corner, taken things into his own hands instead of letting God take the lead. He fisted a hand under his chin.

"Walt needs his granddaughter, Haley, as much as I believe she needs him," he said softly. "Mitch's death crushed him. She could give him hope again. A reason to keep on going."

Haley looked away. "You're putting a lot of responsibility on the shoulders of a seven-year-old."

He moved closer, stopping when he saw her step back. She was right. It hadn't bothered him that his demand to come to South Dakota wasn't fair to Haley, but it wasn't fair to Sarah either. That did bother him.

"All right. I have a proposition for you," he said. "You come first. Get to know Walt and my mother and judge for yourself."

Haley pulled her tattered courage around her like a piece of shredded cloth. It was a fair request. Better than the strong-arm tactic he'd been using. A flicker of hope lit her heart then suspicion edged her closer to caution.

"You must have a lot of confidence in your family's ability to change my mind. What's your angle, Sinclair?"

"No angle, Haley."

"If there's no angle, then there's something I want in return."

A hint of admiration lit his eyes. "I'm listening."

"I'll come for a week. And if at week's end I feel Sarah will be hurt by knowing these people, it's my call to make as her mother and you'll let us both go."

Haley could have milked a cow in the silence that followed. His gaze never left her face. She held it, challenge for challenge, in spite of her fear.

He gave a curt nod. "You're a hard woman."

"When the well-being of my daughter is concerned, I am."

"All right."

"How do I know you'll keep your word?" she asked.

"How do I know you'll keep yours—or be fair in your judgment?" he countered. "It seems we've reached a point where we have to trust each other. At least a little." He hesitated a moment, then held out his hand. "We have a deal?"

Haley felt the envelope bunched in her left hand. She took his hand with her right and felt a shudder run through her body. Sarah mustn't know the truth. Tainted blood money or not, Jared had given her the funds to disappear with Sarah, if it came to that. Accepting his invitation to go to the ranch would buy her time. That was enough because the truth was, she would never, ever subject Sarah to Mitch's family.

Chapter Five

Two days later, Jared sat in the kitchen of his South Dakota ranch watching his mother, Adele, vigorously scrub a plate that he suspected wasn't all that dirty. His mother's response concerning Haley and Sarah had been guarded. He hadn't told Walt yet, more at his mother's insistence than anything else.

"I'm not sure what you hope to accomplish having Haley come here, Jared. This could get ugly."

"Or not," Jared said. That he was very aware of Haley as a woman was undeniable, but maybe that's what had gotten Mitch into trouble. "You don't think this could be good for Walt?"

"Maybe. But until Haley is done judging us, I'd rather Walt not know who she is or why she's here." Adele dried her hands and turned around. "Keep your friends close but your enemies closer? If that's how you're viewing this, son, you're doing it for the wrong reason. If you're going to press this issue of incorporating Haley and Sarah into this family, you need to be looking at what's possible in Haley, not what's lacking."

Jared swirled the cold coffee around the mug and shifted uncomfortably. He was looking for a reason to blame Mitch's death on something other than God's timing. It was easier to blame someone else than accept that God would take Mitch when he was finally at a place he could do the most good. One day, it would be okay. Just not today.

Adele crossed the room and touched his shoulder. "Whatever happened between Mitch and Haley, he left her to raise a child on her own. Jared, that's devastating."

Jared dropped his gaze. He hadn't looked at it in that light. His mother was right. It's what his father had done. If anyone understood Haley and her reasons for doing what she did, his mother would.

"I don't doubt Haley loves Sarah," Jared said, remembering her whispered prayer in the barn. "I just think there's more she hasn't told us. The rest of us deserve to love Sarah, too."

Jared's conscience nudged. Was God using Haley to force him to deal with his own judgmental spirit? He'd seen something while watching her with the pup. She'd been vulnerable, raw with hurt. He didn't want to believe she was the calculating monster he'd made her out to be in his mind. Indecision divided his loyalty. He fisted his hands.

How could he lead others to faith if he placed his

need for justice above Haley's need for God or above his trust that God would make all things just in His own way and time?

"Haley needs to see that we're not bad people."

"I agree, but I'm worried how all this is going to affect Walt," Adele said.

Jared patted her hand. "I would never do anything to hurt Walt, you know that." He placed his hands on her shoulders. "All of us need to heal."

"Even Haley?" Adele asked.

Jared nodded. "Even Haley."

"Then I trust that what you're doing is honorable, Jared. *If* it's the real reason you're doing it," Adele said. Her dark eyes probed his. "Have you examined your own heart and prayed hard about this?"

Jared's conscience pricked. He'd made this deal on the tail of a whim, because he'd glimpsed Haley's pain, but his mother had given him a lot more to think about. No matter which way he looked at bringing Haley here, it still felt right.

"She'll see we're good for Sarah and Sarah's good for us. Walt can have a piece of Mitch to hold onto, and maybe Sarah can help Walt through this dark place he's in right now."

Adele pressed her lips together. "You speak of Sarah. But who will help Haley, Jared? You seem to forget that God doesn't renovate, He recreates. A child is easy to love, but if you find out you're wrong in your assumptions about Haley, are you prepared to support her instead of antagonizing her?"

Jared's mind floundered. His tunnel vision hadn't broadened to include that, but if helping Haley face her monsters is what it took for Sarah to come…

"I guess I will."

"Then you might start by dropping this investigating." Adele crossed back to the sink and folded the dish towel. "Walt isn't well, Jared. I don't want him hurt. I want it clear that I don't want Walt to know about Sarah yet. Not until we know for sure what Haley plans to do. Do you really plan to let them go if that's what she decides?"

Jared looked away. "I hope it won't come to that."

Adele shook her head and sighed. "I expect we'll be doing a powerful lot of praying in the next week. What time is she coming?"

"Late this evening."

Adele's brow wrinkled. "I guess I'd better get busy." She headed toward the stairs, then turned. "Jared. You're certain about this?"

"Given the information I have to work with, I'm as certain as I can be." He watched her leave and brushed a hand across his eyes then picked up the phone and called Sam McIntosh. This could all backfire and hurt the people he loved most. All because he hadn't let God take the lead. Jared bowed his head.

Lord, God. I should have asked for Your guidance. I'm sorry. You said all things work together for good. Please work this out for good.

A half hour past Hot Springs, South Dakota, Haley pulled onto a narrow two-lane road. She set

Jared's directions on the seat, saw her hand shake and swallowed hard.

"Pull it together, Haley. It's just a week."

She'd banked the money and researched an escape for Sarah and herself. She had a plan. After they were settled, somehow, someway, she'd get word to Hap.

At the end of the road, a huge barn surrounded by a white fence came into view. A low-roofed bunkhouse was attached to one side of the barn. Not far away, a sprawling two-story log house nestled in a clearing of towering pines that resembled castle guards. Potted plants swayed in the breeze caught by the wide veranda.

Haley sucked in a breath and swallowed down a feeling of homecoming. If this had been any place other than Jared's she would have loved it—and so would Sarah. Sarah assumed that Haley had taken a quick job that required her to leave immediately. While the assumption wasn't entirely true, it wasn't a lie.

Hap wasn't happy either, but he knew why and where she was going and had once again told her to be up front with Jared about Mitch. The truth hurts, he'd said, but it's the lie that leaves the scars. It seemed her whole life revolved around half-truths. She hated it. But the alternative was much worse. What had happened to the level-headed young woman of yesterday?

The truth will set you free. The words whispered from deep in her memory.

Anger knotted inside her. The truth would destroy

Sarah. Haley stopped the truck, shut off the engine and got out. Jared opened the front door and stepped onto the veranda, followed by a slender elderly woman with a riot of silver curls framing her striking features. She walked off the porch with a spry step that defied her age. Jared followed.

"You must be Haley," she said. "I'm Adele Jessup, Jared's mom." Her dark eyes mirrored Jared's.

Haley gazed uncomfortably from Jared to Adele. "I hope my being here isn't an inconvenience, Mrs. Jessup."

"Call me Adele, dear. Everyone does. And you're welcome here as long as we're clear that I don't want my husband hurt any more than you want your daughter hurt. Walt doesn't know. He just thinks you're a friend of Mitch and Jared and you're here on a short stay. Unless you plan on letting Sarah be a part of our family, I don't want him to know anything else."

Blunt and to the point, just like Hap. Adele's warm smile took the bite out of her words.

"I don't want anyone hurt, either," Haley said.

She felt Jared's hands on her shoulders. For a brief instant, a feeling of being protected consumed her. She clawed her way through the ridiculousness of that emotion and pulled her suitcase from the truck bed, shying away from Jared's touch. The chill of loneliness followed. Jared reached for the handle, his hand brushing hers.

"I'll take that," he said.

"Afraid I might bolt?"

"Yes." He smiled, softening the words.

He seemed more relaxed than she'd ever seen him. But why wouldn't he be? He was in home ground. She was the intruder.

Haley bit back a retort. She didn't want to make a scene in front of Adele. Instinctively, she liked Adele Jessup, though that feeling hadn't been tested. Could she believe Jared? He was a man, and men lied. Mitch had lied. Look where that landed her. But Jared wasn't Mitch. They didn't share blood.

Adele's watchful eyes held questions she was too polite to voice. "Walt wanted to be here, but he's had a bout with his blood pressure again. His medication makes him sleep, so I doubt you'll meet him tonight."

Haley released a breath. Pardoned. Reprieved. Stayed. She didn't have to face Mitch's father tonight. The reason didn't matter.

"I've got some things in the barn to finish up," Jared said. "I'll just be a few minutes." He set the suitcase on the porch.

His gaze caught Haley's. She couldn't look away. He turned and disappeared, swallowed up by the deepening shadows.

"You must be hungry," Adele said. "I have turkey sandwiches and tea ready."

"You shouldn't have gone to so much trouble."

"No trouble. It's nice to have another woman in the house. All this testosterone gets a bit overwhelming at times."

Haley's pulse jumped, throbbing like an old wound that ached on a rainy day. The vision of Mitch abandoning her behind the carnival booth rose to the surface. She stumbled on the step, let go of Adele's arm and gripped the handrail. Coming here was a mistake.

Adele swung the front door open. "Welcome to our home." She ushered Haley inside.

The focal point from the doorway was a massive moss rock fireplace. Family pictures encased in traditional western frames graced the halved log serving as a mantle.

Haley focused on a picture of Mitch. One arm was linked with Jared's, the other with an older man she guessed was Walt Jessup. She stopped and stared at the pictures. She was doing the one thing she'd vowed never to do—walking into Mitch's world of her own free will.

Adele's gaze followed Haley's. "This was taken a few weeks before Mitch died," she said.

Haley's heartbeat drummed in her ears.

A few months before I killed him.

That infernal voice refused to be silenced. She wanted to crush it between her hands and push it away. She hadn't wanted Mitch to die, but she hadn't wanted him to live either. She just wanted him to leave her alone.

"I'm sorry for your loss," Haley said. "My Pop died a few years ago. It's hard to lose someone you love."

Adele touched the frame, then she turned and

smiled. "We did love Mitch, but he wasn't perfect. We know that, Haley. I'm sorry he hurt you."

Like Hap, Adele inspired confidences. Haley longed for a woman to confide in, to trust. Her chest tightened. She waited for the bottom to fall out of her world, much like it had when she knew she was pregnant with Sarah, but she remained oddly grounded. Her confidence rose a notch.

"If you ever want to talk, I'm a good listener," Adele said.

Haley smiled. Would Adele feel the same if she knew about Mitch? Would any of them? The answer shouldn't matter, but it did. Guilt poked her like a hot iron. She hated Mitch for what he'd done. She should hate his family, too. But she didn't.

She followed Adele to the kitchen, her eyes sweeping the wide ceiling beams. A huge wagon wheel light fixture hung from the center beam in the great room. In the adjoining dining room, an antler chandelier hung over an antique oak table. Western art graced knotty pine walls and bronze sculptures adorned hand-carved end tables. Recessed light gave the room a cozy, relaxed feel.

Even the kitchen was done with a modernized version of an antique stove and refrigerator, much like the ones she'd seen at the log home show she and Hap had attended a few years ago in Denver.

"You have a lovely home," Haley said. "Did you and Walt design and build it yourself?"

Adele smiled and motioned toward the breakfast

nook where the table was set for two. Warmth tugged inside Haley. She shoved it back. Feeling homey about this place was something she couldn't afford. She sat down while Adele poured tea into the glasses. The kitchen door opened, drawing their attention.

"Actually, Jared did," Adele said.

"Did what?" Jared said, setting Haley's suitcase on the floor and closing the door.

"Designed and built this house," Adele said.

"Oh." He glanced at Haley.

A smile lit his eyes. Her breath hitched. "You never said this was your house." It hurt to breathe. She thought she was coming to Sarah's grandfather's house, not Jared's.

"The place is a family project," Jared said, avoiding Haley's eyes. "We all worked on it."

Adele motioned to the chair next to Haley and Jared slid into it. "Eat, you two. I'm sure Haley's exhausted and needs rest."

Jared offered thanks. Haley bowed her head, uncertain what to make of this man. When he was finished, Adele busied herself at the sink.

"Jared sank everything into this place. He just keeps us here because he thinks we're too old to take care of ourselves," she said, laughing. "He did the same with Mitch, always looking out for him, fixing things."

Haley met Jared's gaze across the table. If his intent was to fix her, too, he could think again. She wasn't broken.

"So this is a what's mine is yours thing," she said.

"Is that so bad?" Jared asked. "It's important to have family close." His gaze challenged her.

"I suppose that depends on the family," Haley said, picking the crust off her bread. "This is a beautiful place. You do good work."

"Thank you," he said, breaking eye contact.

Adele finished at the sink, then brushed a kiss on Jared's cheek. "If you two don't mind, I think I'll check on Walt and turn in. Tomorrow's going to be busy. Jared, don't forget the afternoon riding session."

"I haven't forgotten," Jared said. "Maybe Haley can help."

"I'm sure the children would like that. If you don't mind," Adele added, smiling at Haley.

"I don't mind. You'll have to tell me what's expected," Haley said grateful for anything that would occupy time.

"Jared can fill you in, dear. Good night, Haley. I'll look forward to getting to know you better." She headed out the kitchen and up the stairs.

Haley finished her sandwich and took a sip of tea, holding the chilled glass between her hands. Jared watched her, but she had no idea what was going on behind those dark eyes. The room was more confining with Adele gone. Jared seemed closer, more intimidating.

"So what is this riding session about, and what do I have to do?"

"A friend of mine cares for handicapped kids

during the week. Once a week they come here and we let them ride and brush the horses. Does wonders for their sense of independence and accomplishment. Mom's been helping, but with Walt not well and taking a lot of her time, your help would be appreciated."

Haley swallowed hard and fingered the condensation on the glass. This was a side of Jared she'd never expected. She wished she'd seen it first. "I'd be happy to help. I think what you're doing is wonderful," she said. "Pop and I used to clown-up and go to the children's ICU and cancer wards and put on a little act." She smiled at the memory. "It's amazing how little it takes to get a child's mind off their troubles."

She lifted her gaze and found him watching her. The glass slid from her fingers, shattering as it hit the table.

Jared reached for a dish towel, sopping up tea before it spilled to the floor. "Are you okay?"

"I'm fine. I'm so sorry," Haley sputtered. "I must be more tired than I thought." She reached for the shattered pieces, cutting her hand on a jagged edge.

Jared pulled a handkerchief from his pocket and wrapped the cut. She stared at the blood soaking through the white cloth.

It was impossible to steady her erratic pulse. "I should have been more careful," she murmured.

Jared covered her hand with his, applying pressure to the cut. Her soft skin brushed against his. He had the feeling she wasn't referring to the broken glass but rather letting him glimpse into her life. He'd wanted her vulnerable so she could see she wasn't the only one who had suffered by Mitch's actions. He'd expected toughness. He hadn't expected her fragility to affect him so much. He pulled the handkerchief back and looked at the torn skin. Jared's breath solidified in his throat.

Weariness replaced the spark in Haley's eyes. Morning would make her more guarded—harder to reach. He had to reach her, now, tonight, for Walt's sake.

"Let's go to the bathroom and clean this up," he said.

He led her to the half-bath near the laundry and eased her onto the toilet seat, then pulled out peroxide and bandages. He flushed the wound with warm soapy water, pinched the skin together and patted it dry. She didn't flinch once, almost as if physical pain stanched the emotional.

"This might sting," he said picking up the antiseptic bottle.

He squirted a liberal amount of liquid onto a cotton ball, dabbed the wound and gently blew on the damp skin. Her hand, so small in his, trembled. Her eyes misted, but not a tear fell.

His vow to not become emotionally involved shattered. "I know Mitch hurt you, Haley. I know you don't want to be here or talk about what happened. I was wrong to jump to conclusions, but I'm not sorry you're here." He secured the bandage and stepped back, irritated that he could be drawn to her in spite of everything he thought he knew, yet driven by the

Spirit within him to help. "Letting go doesn't hurt as much as you think—not as much as holding on."

She stood in a flash and walked into the kitchen. "What would you know of letting go?"

"More than you think." He leaned against the bathroom door, arms crossed. "I've walked that path. Like you, I've already seen yesterday, and it gave me a glimpse of what I want for tomorrow. Someday, if you want to listen, I'll tell you my story. Looking inside ourselves is the toughest thing any of us will ever do, but at some point, it's something we all have to face."

"Is that what Mitch did?" she said resentfully. "Did he look inside himself?"

The spark of challenge was back in her eyes. Jared welcomed it.

"I wonder what he saw." she said, lifting her chin.

"I've wondered that myself." Jared leaned against the sink. "Whatever it was, it brought him back to the God of the second chance, and the third and the fourth. God never gives up on us, Haley, and more often than not, He's the only one who can really help us."

"Sometimes it isn't enough." She picked at the bandage. "Thank you for taking care of this. I'll help with the kitchen."

Jared shook his head. "Not this time." He picked up her suitcase sitting near the door. "It's getting late. Let me show you to your room. Tomorrow's a big day."

Her lashes dropped, hiding her eyes. "You mean tomorrow I have to meet Mitch's father."

Jared nodded. His chest tightened. How impulsive

he'd been to put his own plan first. It was too late for regrets. Too late to go back and do it right.

Jared moved through the great room to the stairs. "Walt's a good man, Haley. I hope you'll give him a chance."

They walked up the stairs. Voices murmured in a room at the end of the hall. Jared stopped before they reached it, opened a door and set the suitcase inside.

"I'm across the hall if you need anything," he said, knowing she would die before asking.

She stepped inside and turned around, the haunted look back in her eyes. "How much does Walt know about why I'm here?" she said.

"Only what Mom told him. That you're a friend of mine and Mitch's, and you're here as my guest. I'll see you in the morning."

He headed for the stairs. The patch on Haley's hand was an easy fix for a simple problem, but the one on her heart…. He could see it, knew who caused it, but had no idea how to fix it. He paused to listen for the sound of her door closing. He didn't hear it until he reached the ground floor. His chest pounded. His misgivings increased by the minute. From here on, he would have to guard his own feelings as well as Haley's actions.

Chapter Six

Haley rose from the bedroom chair and massaged her stiff neck while the sun was still a thought on the horizon. She would have gone to bed hours ago but for the driving need to keep torturous nightmares at bay—the darkness before the dawn. Not even her phone call to Hap and his usual optimistic words of wisdom eased the worry.

A sliver of gray light signaled the long night was ending. She released a sigh. A low burning lamp cast her shadow on the wall. The scent of freshly mowed hay drifted through the open window. Outside, a door banged, a gate creaked and a horse nickered.

She had actually prayed for the darkness to linger, but the morning dawned in spite of her prayer. She hadn't expected Him to answer, but she'd hoped.

She inhaled, relishing the brisk morning air. The day was here, and like every day since her fateful meeting with Mitch, she would embrace it and try to

find what was good. A soft thump outside her door
made her jump.

"Haley?" Jared's voice squeezed through the
heavy oak barrier. "I saw your light," he said. "I know
you're up. If you're game, I could use some company
with chores this morning."

Haley glanced toward the door, then the bed. The
clothes she'd slept in were rumpled. Her unpacked
suitcase, still waiting to be relieved of its contents,
lay on top of the coverlet she hadn't slept under. Her
stomach knotted.

"Haley?" His voice was quieter now, almost a
whisper.

"I'm here," she said. "I haven't escaped down
the trellis."

He chuckled. "Good. Do you want to help me
milk some cows or not?"

"Not." She concentrated on the silence beyond
the door, hoping he'd gone.

"Is there a reason we have to talk through the
door?" he said.

Laughter danced in his voice. Haley could almost
picture the ends of his mouth lifting into a smile. A clear
vision of his face forged in her mind. Her pulse jumped.

She caught her reflection in the mirror and
groaned. Yesterday's clothes clung to her skin.
Smudged mascara emphasized the sleepless circles
under her eyes. Her hair hung to her waist in tangled
waves from the braids she'd worn yesterday.

"I'm not presentable, Jared."

"I doubt that's possible," he said. "I think you're just hiding."

She stormed across the room and yanked the door open. "Get over that, will you?" she snapped. "I'm here, aren't I?"

"Yes. You are." His sharp assessing gaze darkened, touched her briefly and shifted to include the room. "You haven't changed," he said. "Good. You're just perfect for doing barn chores. Splash some water on your face and brush your teeth. If we hurry, we can watch the sun rise."

She stepped back, one hand on the doorknob, ready to shut him out. She shouldn't go. One minute he hounded her, wanting justice for Mitch's death, and the next he treated her like she mattered. Who was this man, anyway? Good grief, last night, he'd even apologized, and she didn't have a witness to prove he'd actually done the deed.

"Haven't you had enough of these four walls for one night, Haley?" Jared's low voice sent a shiver down her back. "There's a gorgeous day starting out there. You don't strike me as the kind of woman to miss a minute of it." He leaned against the doorjamb and crossed his arms, watching her in a way that reawakened feelings she didn't wish to explore.

"You have no idea what kind of woman I am," she said. "I'm no slouch."

"Then show me."

The hall shadows deepened his dark eyes to obsidian—eyes that held an earnestness and honesty that she saw when she remembered Pop, or looked at Hap. She swallowed with difficulty and found her voice. "Give me five," she said.

"Three," he countered, "outside the back door."

A few minutes later, she hurried down the stairs to the kitchen, her ponytail bouncing against her back. The fresh scent of lilac soap lingered on her face. Jared waited on the back porch. She stepped outside and caught her breath. Dawn was breaking, bathing the horizon in a red glow. The scenery and colors changed every second. The world was waking up. Much as she hated to agree with Jared about anything, he was right. It would have been a shame to miss this.

He handed her a jacket and motioned her toward the barn, whistling a happy tune. A lively spring lifted his step. She caught his light mood and changed a little, too. Haunting memories faded. For this moment, this instant, she was free. She wanted to bathe in the glow of that freedom. Caution blinked in her brain.

Remember where you are and who he is.

The lightness left her heart, leaving an ache for its absence. She followed Jared into the barn, hanging back a moment to watch a rabbit nibble grass near the fence. Barnyard hens clucked as they pecked for bugs. In the surrounding paddocks, playful foals reared and nipped at each other while their mothers grazed.

"So, which cow do you want?" he asked, coming close behind her. "Gracie or Claire?"

Unnerved by his nearness, Haley sidestepped him, putting distance between them. "Whichever one you don't want," she said, eyeing the two Jersey cows munching hay in their stalls.

"I'll take Claire. You take Gracie." A mischievous smile curved his lips. He handed her a bucket. "I'm warning you, she's ornery."

Haley lifted her chin. "I face bulls for a living, why would one cow intimidate me?"

A shadow crossed his face, then disappeared. "There's a difference between the he's and she's," Jared said.

"Really," she said, refusing to let him goad her.

"She's kick."

"And he's don't?" Haley countered.

Jared nodded toward Gracie's stall. "Okay. We'll see," he mumbled.

"Say again?" Haley gripped the bucket handle.

"I said, we'll see."

"Is there something in particular that sets this cow off?"

Jared shrugged and grinned. "Doesn't take much."

Haley grabbed a milking stool from the corner and eased into the stall, placing one hand on Gracie's rump. The animal mooed and glanced back. Her large brown eyes seemed calm enough, but looks could be deceiving. Gracie's velvety ears twitched back and forth, then she ducked her head into the manger. Haley paused long enough to shoot a look at Jared.

"You gonna stand there all day?" she asked. "Don't you have your own cow to milk?"

His grin widened. "I do. Holler if you need help."

"Not likely," she muttered.

She set the stool beside Gracie's hind legs, placed the bucket in front of the stool, and slid one hand down the cow's hind quarter. She rubbed in slow circles until she came to the soft flank where the leg and thigh met, the juncture where her forehead should rest while her fingers did the work. Gracie mooed and lifted a leg in warning.

Haley smiled. Jared had given her a ticklish cow. This could be tricky, but if that were all she had to contend with, she'd manage. She settled on the stool and glanced over at the other stall. Jared's dark head rested on Claire's flank. His deft hands worked a steady stream of milk from the udders. Each squeeze pull made the muscles along his shoulders ripple. A wild flutter settled in Haley's stomach.

Jared glanced over his shoulder. "Everything okay?"

"Just peachy," she said, resettling on the stool.

It was too easy to get lost in the way he looked at her. She adjusted the bucket, cupped her hands and blew warm air onto her chilled fingers. Gracie continued to munch, one eye rolled in Haley's direction.

"Behave yourself, Gracie, and we'll get along just fine," Haley said.

She massaged the cow's belly, careful to make each move precise while she eased her hand back until she made contact with the massive milk bag.

Gracie's warm, soft skin melded into Haley's fingers. She tugged at the udders and kept her head out of Gracie's flank.

"Done," Jared called five minutes later. "Mom's making butter today so I'll run this to the shed and put it in the separator." He paused beside her. She chanced an upward glance. "I'm impressed," he said. "Gracie's usually dumped her pail and mashed a few toes by now."

Haley smiled in spite of herself. "I take it this was a test, and I passed."

"With flying colors."

"Good for me," she said, returning to the task at hand.

Heat crept up her neck, radiating warmth through her body. She liked the way he made her feel right now, but didn't trust it. He seemed oblivious to the effect he had on her. She needed to keep it that way.

"I'll be back in a few minutes," he said, moving toward the door.

"Don't hurry on my account," she called.

The pail was half full when the barn door opened. Footsteps shuffled through the fresh shavings scattered on the barn floor. Haley's fingers froze. This wasn't Jared. Jared didn't shuffle. She doubted the hired hand did either. That left Mitch's father. She wasn't ready to see him. Not yet.

"Jared?"

The unfamiliar voice sent a tremor through her body.

She stilled her hands and held her breath. If she didn't move, maybe he'd think no one was here. She closed her eyes. Her head shifted, bumping Gracie's flank.

The cow hunched her back and kicked out, spilling the pail. Haley jumped sideways. The tip of the cow's hoof caught her shoulder. Gracie settled and let out a long, low call, then plunged her head back into the manger, content that she'd done what she set out to do. Haley's world spun like a lariat. A man's feeble hands pulled her from the stall.

"Are you all right?" he asked.

Haley looked into Mitch's father's face. He bore little resemblance to the man she had seen in the photos. His shoulders carried an invisible burden, giving him the stooped appearance of a much older man. Worry lines creased the corners of his eyes. His mouth drooped, as though he seldom smiled anymore. His deep gray eyes were flecked with green and reflected sadness laced with concern. Her first instinct was to comfort and reassure him.

"Are you all right?" he repeated. "What was Jared thinking, letting you milk Gracie?"

Haley slumped against the stall post and winced as pain shot through her shoulder. "In all fairness, Mr. Jessup, Jared did warn me. I was proving a point and doing quite well until a few seconds ago."

"I startled you, didn't I?"

Walt's concern was genuine. She forced the tense muscles to relax, then turned toward the sound of a bucket clanging at the other end of the barn. Jared entered looming larger than life in the rising sun's shadow.

"Haley?" His voice, strong and sure, resonated through the barn. In the space of a heartbeat, he was there, lifting her up and setting her on a hay bale. "I'm sorry. I shouldn't have left…."

"I'm okay." She moved away from his arms and scooted to the far side of the bale. "This isn't the first time I've been knocked in the dirt. I'm sure it won't be the last." She rubbed her smarting shoulder. "I have a job to finish."

Walt's bushy brows pulled together. "Absolutely not," he said, glowering at Jared.

"I agree," Jared said. "Shorty can finish."

Pride waged a war inside her. She never left a job unfinished, even one as simple as milking a cow, but Walt's worried face halted her protest. She picked at the hay. Why should it bother her to worry him? This was Mitch's father, Mitch's family. By all that was fair and just, she shouldn't be here.

Jared nodded toward her shoulder. "May I?" he asked. He knelt before her on one knee, his gaze probing hers. Panic shot through her. She broke eye contact and looked over his shoulder.

Jared's touch made her feel strange, almost needy. The last thing she wanted was to need a man, especially one as potent as Jared Sinclair. He was twisting her emotions into a wad of snarled twine. It was getting harder to define what was happening inside her.

"I'd rather you didn't," she said, wishing herself

anywhere but here, at this time, with this man. "Jared, I think coming here was a mistake," she murmured. "I need to go."

"Leave?" Walt asked, disappointment filling his eyes. "But you just got here. Jared said you knew Mitch. I was hoping we'd have time to talk."

Ice spread through Haley's stomach. She pushed her fist into the bale, drawing Jared's attention.

"In due time, Walt," he said.

Jared's gaze held her, the agreement between them bouncing silently between them. She'd promised to be fair, but she felt ill-equipped to handle any time with Walt, especially if it meant talking about Mitch.

Walt moved a few stalls away. "Please stay, Haley. Jared's never brought a young lady home before and I'd like to hear about Mitch." His plea twisted Haley's gut. He thought she was Jared's girlfriend. He thought she and Mitch had just been friends. Bile rose to her throat and with it, a choking fear that now she was here, there was no escaping the inevitable. When the time came to talk about Mitch, and it would, what could she possibly say that would comfort this man?

You could share Sarah.

Haley stiffened. Not Sarah, not yet. She needed to keep Sarah safe—untouched by Mitch's dirty act. Her gaze roamed over Jared's face. "You promised," she said.

"So did you. Be fair."

Warmth and warning filled his eyes, almost as though he willed his strength into her. Every emotion inside her floundered—anger, fear, hope, all caught in a whirling vortex, leaving her unable to discern anything for certain, except the strength he offered and she needed, but could never accept.

"I don't know what to do," she murmured. "I need Hap."

The hushed words sounded far away, like a lost child searching for something familiar. Jared doubted her voiced need was meant for his ears, but rather a thought she hadn't realized she'd spoken.

Their gazes locked, but hers seemed to look beyond the connection. He was losing her again to that place she never let anyone else go, the place that held the key to the woman behind the clown makeup and the pain she thought no one else could see. For the first time he really saw it, and it ripped him in two.

"If you need Hap, I'll bring him," Jared said, resting his hands on her shoulders. "Just say the word."

Her surprised gaze pulled back to include him. "You would do that?"

He brushed a piece of pine shaving from her hair, letting his hand linger on the silky strands. She didn't pull away. "Yes," he said. "I would do that."

The bell outside the kitchen door tinkled, blending with the song of waking birds.

"Breakfast. Come on." Adele's voice called from the porch.

Jared took Haley's hand and pulled her to her feet.

When she looked at him again, her face was unreadable, shutting him out.

She brushed the dirt and straw from her jeans. The emotion of the past few minutes dissolved, annihilating all traces of the vulnerable woman he'd seen, as though within that space, she'd determined something in her mind. She hurried toward the barn entrance, passed Walt and offered a half smile.

"Thank you for saving me from Gracie," she said before stepping into the sunlight.

Jared rammed his hands into his pockets and joined Walt. Together they watched Haley climb the porch steps and disappear into the house.

"There's a lot of hurt locked up in that gal," Walt said, fastening the barn door. "Whatever on earth caused it?"

Jared placed a hand on Walt's shoulder, giving it a gentle squeeze. "I suspect Mitch did."

Walt's shoulders slumped. "Mitch? But I thought Haley was your girl. Whatever could Mitch have done?"

Jared urged Walt toward the house. He didn't know for sure what Mitch had done, but he planned to find out. "Mitch was a mess when they met several years ago," Jared said, avoiding any reference to the Cheyenne incident. "Only Haley knows what happened." Until he knew what Haley planned to do, silence seemed the better part of valor. "It was a bad time for him and for us. I'm sure it was for Haley, too."

Walt shielded his eyes, hiding the worried look

Jared had seen so often during Mitch's runaway years. "Mitch fixed his mistakes," Walt said. "How could he have missed this one?"

It was a question Jared had asked himself many times in the last few days and with no satisfying answer. He stopped at the porch steps. "Maybe he didn't know what to do about this one. Maybe he was trying to figure it out when God took him home. Whatever happened, Haley's hurt is real. We have to make it right."

"You haven't told me everything, have you, son?" Walt said.

Jared sighed. "I don't know everything and the story isn't mine to tell. Trust me on this."

Walt nodded. They climbed the steps and entered the mudroom off the kitchen.

"Hope everyone's hungry," Adele called, handing Haley a bowl of gravy. She set it on the table. Jared wished he knew what was in her heart. Walt deserved the truth, but if Haley chose to take her secret and leave, she would remove forever the last living part of Mitch that Walt would ever have. Jared couldn't let that happen.

A cold knot formed in his stomach. The cost might be more than he'd anticipated, but he'd put her in God's hands, and God was faithful and just. He'd have to trust. And wait.

Walt's eyes softened. "There's more to it than just helping her, isn't there?" Without waiting for a reply, he entered the kitchen.

Jared took a minute then followed. There was more, but to tag it with a definition at this stage would be crazy.

Breakfast seemed to go on forever with Jared and Adele carrying most of the conversation. Jared watched Haley's troubled face. For a long moment, she looked back at him, then pushed her eggs around the plate. Once the meal was finished, she rose and stacked the dirty dishes.

"Leave them, dear," Adele said. "I'll pop them in the dishwasher. There's a nice spot near the stream beyond the paddocks. Why don't you take a blanket and enjoy the scenery for a couple of hours? The quiet and fresh air will do you some good."

"Mom naps in that spot lots of times," Jared said, stacking more dishes near the sink.

Adele waved him away. "I don't nap. I meditate."

"You snore when you meditate?" Jared asked. His comment pulled a smile from Haley, softening her features.

Adele smacked his arm. "Behave yourself," she said.

Haley relaxed. The love in this family reminded her of Hap and Sarah. It was real, not put on for her benefit. Adele's love for Walt manifested in every move, every word. He returned it action and word, with a touch or a smile. What would being loved like that be like? She looked up to find Jared watching her. Dreams disappeared in a wave of fear.

"Haley?" Adele said. "I can show you the trail if you want to go."

"I think…" She pulled her gaze from Jared's. "I think I'll just clean up and make a few phone calls before the kids get here."

"Holler if you need anything," Adele said. "Walt and I will be down here making butter."

"And I'll meet all of you in the barn in a couple of hours," Jared said.

Haley hurried upstairs and cleaned up, then called Sarah. Tears stung her eyes. She should be home, not here. By the time Sarah handed the phone to Hap, Haley couldn't speak. She listened as Hap assured her of his love and prayers. The miles seemed to drift, bringing him closer.

He'd signed off with, "This is your chance to make somethin' good out of somethin' bad. Take it." His voice was gruff with emotion leaving her as raw as the skin on a newly branded calf.

The truth will set you free. The phrase taunted her, ringing in her ears until she wanted to ram her palms against the sides of her head and squeeze them out.

She wanted to close her heart, but the shadow of truth held, letting a sliver of light into the darkness. A car door banged outside, followed by squeals of excited children. She pushed off the bed and headed for the barn.

Chapter Seven

Charity, a six-year-old with Down's Syndrome, latched on to Haley as soon as she crossed the barnyard. Haley put her arm around the child, knelt down and introduced herself.

Jared smiled at them and Haley's chest tightened. She'd have to examine the feelings Jared dredged from her at some point but not now.

"I expected you a half hour ago," he said. "What kept you?"

"Phone," Haley said, swallowing hard.

"Everything okay?" He lead the last horse into the barn and tied him to a stall.

Haley nodded and touched the picture of Sarah she'd tucked into her pocket. Having it close made her daughter seem closer. "What do you need me to do?"

"Line the kids along the fence. This is a one-on-one deal. Soon as Mom and Walt get here we'll let the kids into the stalls and just supervise their work. They know the drill."

Haley rose and Charity slipped her hand into Haley's and smiled, her eyes sparkling. Haley caught Charity's excitement. This wasn't much different from what she and Pop had done in the hospital wards, only these kids weren't bedfast or terminal.

Walt and Adele joined them, each taking sole responsibility for a child. Jared handled each one with care and tenderness tempered with enough firmness to keep them safe. Almost as though they belonged to him. Haley was conscious of him watching her with dark eyes that held a spark of some indefinable emotion. She concentrated on Charity, but every time his eyes compelled her to look at him, her pulse would jump, then another memory invaded the warmth, leaving a coldness in her chest and a longing for something always beyond reach.

The afternoon passed too quickly and soon they were loading the kids back in the van and waving them off. Walt looked exhausted. Adele hurried him off to the house.

"I'll help with dinner," Haley called, setting the last saddle on the rack.

She closed the tack room door feeling invigorated and more aware of Jared than ever before. She liked this new side to him and so far hadn't seen anything in Walt and Adele that raised warnings concerning Sarah. She relaxed her guard a little.

"You were great today," Jared said. "We make a

pretty good team." He headed toward the grain shed, leaving her standing in the warmth of his praise.

Dinner was subdued, the afternoon's physical exertion taking its toll on everyone. Haley helped clear the table and load the dishes, conscious of Jared's closeness. She needed to get away from him for a while, away from feelings that were better left buried, feelings she feared and didn't want to explore.

"If we're done here, I think I'll take a walk," Haley said.

"Good for you, dear. It's a beautiful evening for one," Adele said. "Oh. By the way, Jared, I almost forgot. A Sam McIntosh called. He said to call him. Something about a snag on the investigation you requested?" The question in her voice was reflected in her eyes. "Did we have a problem with something?"

Jared's gaze flew to Haley. The comfortable atmosphere shattered like glass.

"The problem was mine," Jared said. "I'm handling it."

Haley gripped the chair and waited for the bomb to drop. Her nails pressed into the hard oak. Sam hadn't called her with good news, so what kind of snag was there? Certainly not one that would benefit her if Jared was handling it. Had Jared finally gotten her kicked out of rodeo? Circuit life was all she'd known. She couldn't imagine herself in any other livelihood. Maybe that's what Jared wanted—her and Sarah depending on his family. Fatigue faded in a rush of adrenaline, replaced by searing anger.

"Excuse me," she said, heading out the door. "I'll take that walk now." She reached the bottom of the porch steps and bent over, fighting waves of nausea. For a moment the world circled, then stilled. Behind her, the porch door squeaked. Panic welled in her throat.

"Haley, wait." Jared's footsteps plunked on the board steps. Her stomach clenched so tightly she couldn't move. He stepped around her, blocking her way.

"Are you all right?" he asked.

"No," she said, straightening. Her stomach lurched and settled. "I'm not all right. You got what you wanted."

"And that is?"

"The chance to gloat on home territory. Well, go ahead. If you've finished destroying my life, can I go back to whatever is left?"

"Look at me, Haley." She refused, focusing instead on some invisible spot to his left. "Look at me," he commanded, lifting her chin with his finger. She transferred all her anger into one look. "I'm not gloating," he said. "And I am sorry about this. At the time I requested the investigation, I needed to know about Mitch. I didn't know about Sarah."

She raised her chin higher. "But you still needed vindication."

Her arrow hit its target. Jared felt the barb. He had wanted vindication in the beginning. But this was now and things were different. He knew about Sarah and the affect of jumping in where angels fear to tread and not allowing God to lead him had messed up everything.

"Stopping the investigation is out of my hands, Haley. I'm sorry. That's the snap Sam was talking about. We're still working on getting it dropped."

"How big of you. Do it for Sarah, not because it was an accident." Her eyes darkened like storm clouds. "Don't you see what will happen by dropping the investigation now?"

"If it's any consolation, Sam told me from the beginning that the ruling would most likely go in your favor," Jared said, confused by her anger.

"And you went ahead with it anyway. I'm still guilty by assumption. I want my name cleared. Unless you're willing to make a public apology and reinstate my reputation, whatever happens won't be enough. Would you do that? For me? For Sarah?" Her words came faster, her panic more pronounced.

A knot rose in Jared's throat. She was right, but he still wasn't ready to take it that far. He dropped his gaze, ashamed of the doubt still clouding his mind.

"I didn't think so," Haley said. "If they fault me, will you take it further? Send me to jail? It was an accident, Jared, and this is the last time I will defend myself to you."

Watching her unravel pained him. He should have left things in God's hands, but no, he'd jumped the gun and made a mess before he had all the facts. He'd done this too much lately, and God forgive him, he was still doing it.

"You don't have to worry about supporting Sarah, Haley. We'll take care of you both."

Her eyes blazed. "I have a life. It's mine and it doesn't include you. I don't need you or any man to take care of me or my daughter. That's what you were hoping for, wasn't it? You're sorry for lots of things. So am I. Does that qualify you for redemption?"

Jared's anger rose. "No. Does it you?"

Rage shook her. She'd glimpsed parts of Jared that stirred a yearning for things she thought she'd never have. Things that stirred a hope in spite of her circumstances. Reality punched her in the gut. What a fool she'd been to let those feelings creep in. She wanted to hurt him like his doubt hurt her.

"It doesn't qualify either of us," she said lowering her voice. "The truth is you're not sure I didn't let Resurrection kill Mitch, even if you want to believe I didn't. You'll never be certain, will you?"

The truth hit her like a steamroller. Disappointment throbbed like a painful knot inside her. It mattered that Jared believed her. Why, she didn't know. And it mattered more that she believed in her own innocence.

She would always feel responsible, but accepting the truth in her heart as well as her mind released the doubt and some of the guilt. Her own vindication had been a long time coming. She'd never meant to physically hurt Mitch. If anything good had come from being here with Jared, this was it. Maybe, someday, he would believe it, too.

"Tell me about you and Mitch, Haley. Make me

understand how all this fits," he said so softly she almost missed it.

The shame of eight years ago rose to the surface, tearing open old wounds, leaving her raw and vulnerable. "Mitch was a wrong turn I made a long time ago," she said in a low voice. "If I'd wanted to destroy him, I could have done it eight years ago. I didn't."

Jared's tense jaw betrayed his frustration. "Isn't Sarah proof that your relationship wasn't all bad?" His look translated as disappointment. "Most people don't have a child with someone they don't care about."

"Mitch wasn't most people." Haley's heart pounded so hard she was sure he could see it move beneath her shirt. He thought she'd slept with Mitch, then kept the news of Sarah from him. How wrong could he be? She couldn't hold his gaze. If she did, he would see her shame, not Mitch's. Carrying her own cross was so familiar she'd miss it if it wasn't there. Oh, what she wouldn't give to share the load, but not with this man, her enemy's brother.

"You want to know what Mitch gave me," she said, hearing the bitterness in her voice. "I'll tell you. He gave me the gift of looking over my shoulder for the rest of my life." Without waiting for his response, she turned and fled toward the paddocks.

Jared let her go, but her words hung in the air, haunting him, leaving an insinuation that he never knew Mitch at all. Why would she need to look over her shoulder, unless…

Something inside him died. The reflection taking seed in his mind was too awful to contemplate. Mitch at his worst would never do such a thing. He couldn't. Yet Mitch's pained cry came back in a rush of memory.

I've done some awful things.

Every move Haley made said Mitch could have and if he had… Jared fisted his hands. He had wrongly judged Haley in the department of keeping Sarah from Mitch, but not in the incident with Resurrection. If the roles were reversed, how far would he have gone to protect his child? His stomach roiled. There was no way to know for sure what really happened or why. More than ever, in spite of his doubts, he needed to stop judging her at every turn.

Jared shoved the darkness from his mind and headed toward the small office building beside the barn, his troubled thoughts hounding his heels. His mother met him at the door.

"Is Haley all right? She seemed upset about the call."

Jared sat down at his drafting board and stared at the blueprints for the ranch expansion. "I'm afraid I started something I can't undo."

"I'm sorry. I was afraid stopping the investigation wouldn't be so easy."

He studied his mother's face. Her earnest eyes, filled with life and unquenchable warmth, asked questions she wouldn't voice. For the first time it dawned on him that maybe the key to helping Haley lied with his mother.

"Is there something I can do?" she asked.

"Maybe. What do you see when you look at Haley?"

Adele frowned. "I'm not sure I know what you mean."

"What do you see inside her, Mom?"

"I don't have X-ray vision, Jared. I'm not sure a few hours gives me the right to make any kind of assessment."

"Try, Mom. You're a good judge of character. It's important."

Adele grew quiet. "I see a woman in a lot of pain who thinks she doesn't deserve to be loved."

Jared slid a pencil between his fingers, surprised by her answer. "Why do you think she believes that?"

"Just a hunch. Her movements, reactions. Women see these things, but I could be wrong. You've known her longer. You should know better than me." She stepped in front of the desk and stopped. "Jared, if this is related to Haley's relationship to Mitch, this might be something you can't fix. I don't want to see you or Walt hurt."

"I don't want that either."

"You can't rescue the world. Sometimes people have to find their own way."

Jared reflected on his mother's words. "And maybe God puts certain people in our path so He can use us to help them find their own way," Jared said, believing more and more that was what had happened in spite of the circumstances. "Maybe God is using us now to make Haley see that in spite of everything, she is important. If that's the case, then I haven't allowed Him to use me in that way. I've failed."

She patted his arm, then opened the door and stepped outside. "Or not. Just be careful."

After she'd gone, Jared fisted his hands under his chin, then bowed his head. "Lord, God," he murmured. "Help me. I'm lost in this and I don't know what to do. Show me the truth."

A sense of God's peace washed over him, renewing and offering hope. He turned back to the drawing board and finished the sketch.

Night settled over the valley, the full moon reflecting on the shimmering stream. Cold settled around Haley's heart. She'd seen enough of Jared to know he'd backed her into a corner, again. The wind whispered through the pines, touching her cheek like Jared had done not so long ago. He'd put a brand on her, not like Mitch, but a mark just the same. She knew the danger of instant attraction and wouldn't fall into that trap again.

Still, the truth lay closer to the surface than ever before. She'd rather face a rank bull again than the ghost of Mitch. Everything she'd done had been to protect those she loved. If the truth were known, would people look at her and Sarah differently?

Would Jared?

Of course he would. Whatever path she chose, someone would lose. She rose and brushed the tears from her face, then turned toward the house and saw Adele making her way through the brush.

"I was afraid you'd get lost," Adele said. "Beautiful, isn't it?"

Haley nodded.

"I always find such peace here. There was a time I never thought I would."

Haley knew that feeling well, but it surprised her that this calm, together woman would, too. She plunked a rock into the water and edged toward the path. "What happened to make you feel that way?"

"Jared's father." Her quiet voice held no malice, only acceptance for what had been and was no longer.

"I was young. We eloped. Six months later, the reality of being married to a man with a cruel streak sunk in. But I was pregnant with Jared." She paused as if looking back was something she rarely did. "I wish I'd listened to my parents. They saw what I didn't or wouldn't. I would have done anything to get away and spare Jared growing up in that atmosphere."

"How did you make it through?" Haley slowed her step.

"Life got better when I decided God could carry the load better than I could."

"Maybe some people are more deserving of God's favor than others," Haley said.

The touch on her shoulder was gentle. "God doesn't play favorites, dear. If He did, how would anyone trust Him? He loves us all and desires all to come to Him, but the final choice to trust and follow are left up to us."

"Sometimes we choose to follow but bad things still happen," Haley said.

"The world is what it is, Haley. We have to live in it for the present. It's good that we don't see the beginning and the end. We'd evade anything remotely difficult and never grow."

Haley closed her eyes, clearly seeing Sarah's face. "I'm sorry for what you went through," she said. She opened her eyes to find Adele still watching, warmth and understanding in her dark eyes. "What did you tell Jared about his father?"

Adele smiled. "The truth. It's shaded a bit differently when a little boy is five than when he's thirty, though."

"What if…" Haley swallowed. "Why doesn't God stop the bad things before they happen? What if He's responsible for our predicaments and there's no way to fix what happens or make it better?"

Adele's gaze was reflective. "You can always make it better. God isn't in the business of placing His children in predicaments, Haley. We manage that quite nicely on our own. The journey may be rough, but He promises a safe landing."

Haley brushed a hot tear off her cheek. "What if I can't make it through the journey?"

Adele took her hand and squeezed it. "If you're truly God's child, that's impossible. What's troubling you? Can I help?"

"No. No one can. Nothing is right—anywhere."

Haley freed her hands and ran them down her jeans, then stepped onto the path. Adele waited for her to continue, but Haley knew she wouldn't. She longed for someone to share her burden with, someone who could explain what was happening inside her—anyone but Jared's mother, whose warmth and quiet manner encouraged confidences that, if the truth were known, would only tear apart and destroy both their families. The house came into view and she quickened her step. When they reached the porch, Adele stopped.

"There's more to life than surviving, Haley. There's joy and love. You deserve that. Everyone does. I'll see you in the morning."

Haley slipped into the house and hurried up the stairs to her room, avoiding the den where Jared and Walt were bent over a chessboard. Fear and shame clawed at her insides like an old enemy. She didn't want Sarah to know the truth or be torn in relationships or worst of all hate her for Mitch's sin. She didn't want to be here where reminders of Mitch constantly bombarded her and feelings of hearth and home and Jared invaded her thoughts.

The truth will set you free.

She opened her bedroom window and lifted her gaze to the heavens. "Will it set me free?" she whispered. "How can You make this right?"

Haley rose at first light and entered the barn. She grabbed a clean pail and headed for Gracie's stall. The cow was munching hay, which meant Jared must be up, too. She quickly washed the cow's udders and sanitized her hands, then sat on the milking stool and closed her eyes.

She'd never been so tired. Against her better judgment, she asked God for help last night, wrestled with Him for some time with no resolution. Why should He listen to her? She'd abandoned Him, just as He had her, but she'd hoped He would feel some of her desperation and take pity on her.

Instead, exhaustion had riddled her sleep with nightmares of Mitch and visions of Sarah being taken away. She didn't doubt Walt and Adele would love Sarah, as well as materially offer her more than she and Hap ever could. What would happen if she let Sarah come and Sarah didn't want to leave?

Gracie stomped her foot as Haley yanked a little too hard. She eased her grip. It could happen. If Sarah came. Haley ground her teeth. She'd stick with her plan—finish out the week and use the money Mitch had left to take Sarah somewhere safe. Away from the truth about him. Away from Jared.

Away from Sarah's family.

Haley's chest squeezed. She sidelined the voice in her head and finished milking, carried the milk to the mudroom and poured it into the separator, then stepped into the kitchen.

"You're up early," Jared said. "Gracie give you any trouble this time?"

Her heart lurched, then settled back into its natural rhythm. "No. She was fine." Jared was reason enough not to stay. He confused her with memories of the life she'd dreamed of before Mitch. A life lost. There was no future in lost dreams.

He downed a glass of juice, rinsed and set it in the dishwasher. "Thought we might take a ride, if you're interested. Have a bunch of spring colts I'd like you to see."

"I'd like that." She heard Adele and Walt shuffling around upstairs. So far, Walt hadn't cornered her to talk about Mitch. She suspected Jared was responsible for the reprieve. Still, it made her anxious every time Walt was close. "I'll go saddle up."

"Aren't you hungry?" he asked

Haley shook her head. "Show me which horses you want and I'll get them ready while you eat," she said.

Disappointment shaded his eyes. His lips tightened a fraction. "Who are you running from, Haley? Me or Walt?"

"Both," she challenged. "Do you have a problem with that?"

"Yes," he said, joining her by the door, "I do. Come on. I'll show you where everything is."

A few minutes later, Haley tied the saddled horses to the fence and headed for the house. She entered the mudroom and grabbed her hat from the hook.

"Ready when you are," she said stepping into the kitchen. To her dismay, Walt and Adele had joined Jared.

Jared looked up from the sink and smiled. "Give me a minute."

"You two go on," Adele said, shooing Jared away.

He placed his cereal bowl in the dishwasher. Haley's chest tightened. This could have been her life, or something similar, if only Mitch… She shook the memory loose.

"Morning, Haley," Walt said, pouring a cup of coffee. "You better eat. Jared has a way of making a short ride into an all day thing."

"I'm not much on breakfast," she replied, backing into the mudroom. "I'll be fine."

Walt challenged her comfort zone, but the fault was hers, not his. She could feel the love in this room and wanted to be included, but Mitch made that impossible.

"I'll bring the horses up," she said.

Jared's black brow arched, mocking her desire to run. She hadn't fooled him. "Right behind you," he said. "Think you could go a little faster?"

Haley ignored the jibe and pushed the porch door open as the phone rang. Adele answered. Silence followed. Then Adele's choked, "Sarah, is everything all right?" made Haley spin around. She pushed past Jared and rushed toward Adele, who cradled the phone like it was something precious.

"Your mother's right here," Adele said, her voice hushed. "Just a minute."

Haley resisted the urge to yank the phone from Adele's hands. Hap would never give Sarah this number. They'd call her cell. Except she'd forgotten to plug it in last night. Something must have happened. Fear twisted her heart.

Adele handed the receiver to Haley with shaking hands. Her stricken gaze bounced from Walt to Jared, then a tear slid down Adele's face.

"It's Sarah," she said in a choked whisper.

Haley grabbed the phone then sank into a chair, her knees shaking.

"Sarah, it's Mom. Are you okay? Is Hap okay?"

She felt Jared's hand on her shoulder, strong, re-assuring, and welcomed it.

Haley heard Sarah's muffled, "We're fine," and released her breath. Sarah's panicked voice kept talking, but Haley barely heard. Sarah was all right. Nothing else mattered.

Sarah explained that Haley had forgotten to fill out the insurance form for the gymkhana entry and she couldn't ride in the horse competition without it. Hap couldn't find the information and wouldn't call the emergency number Haley had left, so she'd called instead. Haley gave her the number and had her repeat it. She held the phone close, wishing it would bring Sarah closer than just the sound of her voice.

"I thought something bad had happened, Sarah. Don't ever scare me like that again," Haley said. "I love you," she murmured. She hung up, then raised her head to find three pairs of eyes watching her. Her pulse raced, feeling like she'd just been roped and yanked from the saddle.

Adele was dabbing tears from eyes that held a trace of panic as they passed from Jared, to Walt, to her. Jared's face was grim. Walt's puzzled look passed between the three of them. He placed an arm around Adele, studied them all for a brief moment, then looked at Haley. His intense stare made her want to run.

"Haley. Who is Sarah?" he said, breaking the silence. "And why would talking to her upset my wife like this?"

Chapter Eight

Haley lifted her chin, letting her gaze rest on each person.

"Sarah's…my daughter," she said, feeling the noose tighten around her.

"I get that," Walt said. "But why didn't you bring her with you and why would talking to her make Adele cry?"

Haley's gaze bounced between Adele and Walt, then rested on Jared. No help there. Omitting the truth had worked until now. But this was too big to shade over. Walt's eyes seemed to look right into her soul to the secret she'd kept from him.

"Jared?" Adele said. "I don't think…"

"It's time," Jared said, shaking his head. He took Walt's elbow.

Haley backed away. She was the outsider, the one who didn't belong, but Sarah's call had opened the gate and there was no turning back now.

Get 2 Books FREE!

Steeple Hill Books, publisher of inspirational romance fiction, presents

Love Inspired

A series of contemporary love stories that will lift your spirits and reinforce important lessons about life, faith and love!

FREE BOOKS!
Get two free books by acclaimed, inspirational authors!

FREE GIFTS!
Get two exciting surprise gifts absolutely free!

HURRY!

Return this card today to get **2 FREE Books** *and* 2 **FREE** **Bonus Gifts!**

Love Inspired®

YES! *Please send me the 2 FREE Love Inspired® books and 2 FREE gifts for which I qualify. I understand that I am under no obligation to purchase anything further, as explained on the back of this card.*

affix
free
books
sticker
here

313 IDL ERV5   113 IDL ERVH

FIRST NAME	LAST NAME

ADDRESS

APT.#	CITY

STATE/PROV.	ZIP/POSTAL CODE

Steeple Hill Reader Service — Here's How it Works:

Accepting your 2 free books and 2 free mystery gifts places you under no obligation to buy anything. You may keep the books and gifts and return the shipping statement marked "cancel." If you do not cancel, about a month later we will send you 4 additional books and bill you just $4.24 each in the U.S. or $4.74 each in Canada, plus 25¢ shipping & handling per book and applicable taxes if any.* That's the complete price and — at a savings of at least 15% off the cover price, it's quite a bargain! You may cancel at any time, but if you choose to continue, every month we'll send you 4 more books, which you may either purchase at the discount price or return to us and cancel your subscription.

*Terms and prices subject to change without notice. Sales tax applicable in N.Y. Canadian residents will be charged applicable provincial taxes and GST. Offer not valid in Quebec. All orders subject to approval. Books received may not be as shown. Credit or debit balances in a customer's account(s) may be offset by any other outstanding balance owed by or to the customer. Please allow 4 to 6 weeks for delivery. Offer available while quantities last.

If offer card is missing write to: Steeple Hill Reader Service, 3010 Walden Ave., P.O. Box 1867, Buffalo, NY 14240-1867

BUSINESS REPLY MAIL
FIRST-CLASS MAIL   PERMIT NO. 717   BUFFALO, NY

POSTAGE WILL BE PAID BY ADDRESSEE

STEEPLE HILL READER SERVICE
3010 WALDEN AVE
PO BOX 1867
BUFFALO NY 14240-9952

NO POSTAGE
NECESSARY
IF MAILED
IN THE
UNITED STATES

"There's something I need to tell you," she said. "It's about Sarah."

She caught Jared's warning look, Adele's worried frown. Walt edged forward. His face flushed. "What am I missing here?"

Haley's insides shook. She leveled her gaze on Jared, then Walt. "It's about Sarah and Mitch," she said.

For a moment Walt seemed suspended, then his face turned red. Words formed on his lips, but he couldn't get them out.

"What about Sarah and Mitch?" he finally choked.

"I…Mitch…" Her voice warbled. "Sarah is Mitch's daughter. Mitch's and mine."

A strangled cry escaped Walt's mouth. His arms lifted, then dropped. He was getting more and more agitated. Blurting it out like this wasn't what she'd wanted. But few things in her life were what she'd wanted. Walt didn't deserve to be hurt any more than she deserved what his son had done. She looked to Jared but he was concentrating on Walt's blotched features and shaking legs.

"Mom, why don't you get his meds," Jared said.

Walt waved them both away. "No. I can't think when I take them. I need to think."

Haley waited for him to blast her.

"I have a granddaughter," he said, awe filling his voice. His eyes misted. "Mitch's girl." His gaze met hers, accusing. "Why didn't you tell us?"

The shame of that day overwhelmed her. "I couldn't. Mitch was…he was…I wanted him out of my life. And Sarah's." She ran her hands across her jeans, then reached inside her shirt pocket and pulled out the picture of Sarah that she'd kept close to her heart since coming here. "I'm sorry," she said, holding it out.

"Haley, I don't think he's ready," Adele began. Her dark eyes flashed a warning.

"It's too late for that now," Walt said pulling away. "Are you all in on this? Am I the only one who didn't know?" He reached for the photo, then gasped. "Spitting image of her daddy." He inhaled sharply, then grabbed Jared's arm and pitched forward, crushing the photo to his chest.

Jared lifted him and carried him to a chair, Adele right behind.

Haley felt more alone than she'd ever felt in her life. Her stomach lurched. She'd watched Mitch die and lived with the knowledge every day that had it not been Mitch, she may have acted faster. Jared was right. She was in some part responsible. But Walt... She'd never forgive herself if something happened to him. Neither would Jared and Adele. How could she face any of them again? She rushed to her truck, pulled the keys from under the seat and drove away.

It was dark when Haley pulled back into Jared's drive and cut the engine. A single, low burning light came from her bedroom window—a beacon in a storm. Walt's crumpled body and Adele's stricken face brought back vivid memories of Mitch lying in the arena. She needed to make sure Walt was all right, to somehow explain without causing him any more hurt.

She got out and rushed for the porch, then caught sight of a huge shape looming along the fence beside the house. Anxiety swamped her. She reached for the doorknob, hoping it wasn't locked.

"Haley, wait."

Jared's voice stopped her cold. He urged the horse into the light and paused beside the porch.

"I shouldn't have run off," she said retracing her steps.

"No. You shouldn't have." His gaze bored into her, stretching her nerves like barbed wire to a post. "Walt asked for you all afternoon. He's afraid you're going to take Sarah and go into hiding. Is he right?"

Heat crept up Haley's neck. She was grateful that her back was to the light so he couldn't see the truth in his words.

"Walt's okay then?"

"Yes. Are you going to answer my question?"

"No."

She could feel his agitation. "I think you just did. So is Walt why you came back?"

She nodded.

Jared crossed his arms on top of the saddle horn and leaned forward. "Are you prepared to answer his questions without putting any more stress on him?"

"Do I have a choice? You're the one who forced me to come here, so don't put all the blame on me. You wanted him to know. Now he knows."

"I wanted Sarah to come with you. Look, Haley, we can play the blame game all night and never resolve it. Walt knows, so you know what comes next. And I'm warning you, it isn't running."

She moved to the horses side and absently stroked the powerful neck. "I don't want to hurt Walt any more than you want to see him hurt. I don't think I can finish this."

"I will never be finished, Haley. Not now. You closed the door on that."

She met his gaze and backed away. "You have a right to be angry with me, but my first consideration is still my daughter. And she doesn't know."

Jared heaved a sigh. "Then it's time she did." He shifted his weight.

"You messed things up." Her voice sounded small, even to her own ears.

Jared's eyes softened. "And your method of delivery is a little unorthodox."

"I'm sorry." Panic rushed to her throat. "I thought something had happened. I should…talk to Walt and Adele now." The horse lowered his head. She rubbed the sensitive pressure points behind his ears wishing Jared would dismount and not tower over her like a lion waiting for a meal.

"When you do, do you think you could manage to be a little less diplomatic?"

Her eyes flew to his face. He smiled and she realized he was trying to lighten the tension. She relaxed a little, then scuffed her toe in the dirt. "I failed Tact and Diplomacy 101," she countered.

Jared chuckled. The sound stirred her heart. "Wait until morning. The doctor gave Walt something to help him sleep and Mom won't leave him tonight."

"She must think I'm awful."

"She thinks you've been hurt, but her first concern is about Walt."

"They must really love each other," Haley said, shifting her gaze to the house. "They're lucky to have that." Longing stirred her heart. She heard Jared dismount, then move behind her, the connection between them so tangible she could barely breathe.

"Ride with me," he said.

It wasn't a question. Uncertainty and fear tightened her chest. She stepped around the horse, putting the animal between herself and Jared, then moved toward the barn. She didn't want to ride with Jared, but the alternative of being alone with her thoughts wasn't appealing either.

"Mitch didn't know about Sarah," she said quietly. "I could have found him. I didn't want to."

"Why not?"

The horse nickered, adding to the sounds of crickets, hoot owls and cattle mooing. The scent of Adele's rose garden filled the night air. "Because he was in a bad place and didn't deserve her. I wanted her in my world. Not his."

She rushed ahead, needing space. Jared wasn't Mitch. But the mocking voice of doubt wouldn't be silenced. Nothing good could come from this. She needed to hold Sarah tight and feel the love between them and lay to rest this want for something more. Something she wasn't able to give. Sarah was enough. Whatever this thing was between her and Jared, she had to stop it.

She spun around, nearly smashing into his chest. He dropped the reins and placed his hands on her shoulders, then stared into her eyes for what seemed an eternity. She stepped back. The warm night air separated them.

"You don't have to do everything by yourself, Haley. And it isn't wrong to want something more for yourself either." No anger filled his eyes, only endless questions and a desire to know the truth.

"I'm doing the best I know how, Jared. I know better than anyone that how a girl feels about herself is tied to how she feels about her father," she said, steering the conversation back to Sarah. "All I know about Mitch are things that I don't want Sarah to know."

"Maybe that's why God put us in each other's paths."

Haley bristled. "You hunted me down. I don't think God had anything to do with it."

"I'm sure He did. If you can't find anything good about Mitch, then let us help. You only saw the bad. We saw both. We saw him straighten his life out. Don't deny Sarah the good things."

Haley brushed away an escaping tear. Words stuck in her throat. Jared wasn't saying anything Hap hadn't said already.

"To know what is right and not do it is as bad as doing wrong," Jared said. His low voice took the sting out of his words. "You know this is right."

She turned back to the barn, flipping on the light inside the door. She quickly saddled a horse while Jared watched. They'd gone through a gamut of emotions this day, shock, anger, compassion, longing, yet she sensed something new, like a door opening, an unseen opportunity, but the what and why were shaded.

"What are you afraid of, Haley?"

She mounted and joined him outside, letting her horse fall into step on the gravel road. "I'm afraid of not ever being normal." She regretted the words as soon as she said them.

A smile tugged at his mouth. "I got the feeling you think normal is highly overrated. You're a bullfighter. Not exactly a job you'd look for in the classifieds."

The laughter left his eyes as the last light from the barn faded and the ranch house disappeared from view.

"Mitch was a fool to let you go," he said.

His voice was soft as the summer breeze, his words a vivid reminder of the normal life she wanted and would never have—all because of Mitch. Mitch hadn't let her go. He'd used her and cast her aside. She could never come to any man pure and undefiled. Not now. She let the night wash over her, the darkness covering her shame. The ride was a silent one, both she and Jared lost in their own thoughts. It ended much too soon. When they returned to the barn she unsaddled her horse and tossed some feed in the stall.

Jared ran a brush over his horse and latched the gate. "I appreciate the gift you're giving Walt—and what it's costing you."

She ducked her quivering chin. "I haven't agreed to bring Sarah yet. I'm still not convinced it's the right thing."

"It's the only thing," he said, a hint of anger back in his voice. "Don't take this from him."

Haley stepped out of the barn into the moonlight. Hap would know. She'd talk to Hap, then decide.

Jared's hands guided her in a half circle, his face inches from her own. She felt the pull toward him in spite of all that had passed between them. It had been so long since she'd been alone with any man but Pop and Hap. She wanted the fear to go away. She wanted back all that Mitch had stolen and destroyed. She wanted normal—to be here, drinking in the scent of earth and horse, with Jared—free from the chains that had bound her for so long.

She wanted to not be alone, to love and be loved, to be that special someone like Adele was to Walt, and feel protective arms around her and know the brush of a man's lips without knowing the terror that followed. If she could do that, with Jared of all people, maybe there was a chance she could grow whole again.

She lifted her gaze from his shirt button, following the line of his throat to his lips, then his eyes.

Something smoldered in their depths. She caught her breath, forcing back her rising panic.

His calloused hand brushed a wisp of hair from her face and lingered on the pulse throbbing in her neck. She steeled herself for his head to dip, for his lips to touch hers. Instead, he planted a well-placed kiss on the top of her head.

"Good night, Haley. Dream well. I'll see you in the morning."

He walked back into the barn leaving her uncertain whether to be disappointed or pleased.

Ten days later, Haley arrived back at Jared's with Sarah in tow. She hoped he'd kept his word in seeing that Walt and Adele were gone a few hours before this meeting took place.

Haley's discussion with Walt and Adele after her outburst about Sarah had been tense—the most difficult interview she'd ever had, but she'd managed to answer Walt's questions, leaving his memories of Mitch in a favorable light.

There was no doubt both Adele and Jared suspected her feelings ran much deeper than she was willing to voice, but they'd both kept silent. She sensed Adele's protectiveness of Walt had shifted their relationship in a different direction.

Haley pulled into the drive and glanced at Sarah. So far Sarah had taken everything in stride, but Haley knew her daughter well enough to notice the unusual quietness that had settled over her the last few hours.

How she wished Hap had accepted Jared's invitation, or better yet, let her take Mitch's money and run, but he'd left her with a whispered, "You start runnin' now, you'll never stop, and Sarah's the one who'll pay. I ain't goin' anywhere. I'll be right here when you need me."

Jared shut the barn door and walked toward them as the truck rolled to a stop. Late afternoon sun cast a long shadow before him. Haley's heart skipped. She had missed him more than she'd realized. That in itself didn't bode well for her.

"Is he really my uncle?" Sarah asked, craning her neck to see over the dash. A hint of excitement returned to her voice.

Haley nodded. Telling Sarah about Mitch without putting him in a bad light had been hard. Telling her that her father had died in a rodeo accident was harder. She'd expected a barrage of questions about Mitch, but Sarah's only reaction was joy that now she had a real family with relatives like her other friends.

"He looks like Superman," Sarah said. "'Cept his eyes are dark. He's got nice eyes, Mom. Don't you think?"

"I suppose he does," Haley said, trying not to remember how they glistened in the moonlight, then softened before his lips burned the kiss into her forehead.

Jared left her wanting more of the one thing she feared she'd never achieve—a relationship unfettered by pain and bad memories.

Sarah opened the door and jumped out, her wide-eyed gaze absorbing everything at once. Haley followed, grateful that Sarah was such a well-adjusted seven-year-old in spite of her apprehensions. If only she, too, possessed the same resiliency.

Sarah's gaze lingered on the house. Haley sensed it draw Sarah, just as it had drawn her. Fear jabbed into her heart.

"Is this where my dad lived?" Sarah asked.

Haley winced at the word choice. Mitch had never been a dad. "I suppose he did for a while," she said.

Jared joined them and squatted down to Sarah's level. He extended his hand and she took it. "Welcome to the Silver Quarter, Sarah. Your grandparents didn't think you'd be here until later. They went into town to take care of a few things."

Haley relaxed a little. Jared had kept his word.

"Would you like to see your room?" Jared asked Sarah.

"My room? My very own room? Here?"

Sarah's face lit up. Haley shifted uncomfortably. This place offered more than she could ever hope to give her daughter. When the time came to leave, what if Sarah didn't want to go?

"Sarah and I can share my room," Haley said.

Jared's black brow lifted. "You don't have to do that." He rose, his face only a foot from hers. "There's plenty of room for everyone."

Haley's gaze fastened on his lips, suspending the breath in her lungs. "I know that," she murmured.

"Hey, you two. I'm here," Sarah said, pushing them apart. "I feel like the middle of an Oreo cookie."

Jared threw back his head and laughed. The sound went straight to Haley's soul and settled. To an outsider looking on, they could have been a loving, happy family. She wanted that—to share her life with someone. How could she fix what Mitch had taken away?

Jared pulled the suitcases from the pickup bed. "I take it Hap decided not to accept our invitation."

"He thought it would be easier for Walt if he wasn't around," Haley said, feeling his absence.

"But not easier for you."

Haley shrugged her shoulders. "I'm used to not easy." His perception unsettled her. She pulled her purse from the truck and shut the door.

"Let's get you two settled," Jared said. "Which is it, Sarah? You want to room with your mom or not?"

"Not," she said, wrinkling her nose. "Mom talks in her sleep and has nightmares. Sometimes she screams. Hap has to go and wake her up."

Sarah glanced up at Haley. She felt Jared's curious gaze, but couldn't bring herself to look at him. He was part of the reason for her restless nights.

"Is it okay if I have my own room?" Sarah asked.

"Sure," Haley replied, her voice shaking.

"Then follow me," Jared said, heading toward the house.

He hadn't missed the range of emotions racing across Haley's face—surprise, hurt, but mostly anxiety. The nightmare revelation was something new. Jared swallowed, then tightness closed his throat. Nothing was certain, but his suspicions about the life Mitch led before he'd repented and accepted God's forgiveness hounded him.

Sarah's chatter filled the hallway. He led the way upstairs, trying to imagine Haley's fear of walking into Mitch's home territory, of losing Sarah to all the things Walt and Adele could and would shower on her, things she couldn't provide. She wanted to protect Sarah and herself. He wanted that, too. They'd come a long way since that first meeting at the Cheyenne rodeo grounds. If he'd relied more on God's leading than his own actions, would things have been smoother for Haley and his doubts about Mitch's death put to rest?

He paused at the bedroom across from his, the one Haley had occupied ten days ago, then moved to the room right next to it and opened the door. "These rooms have a connecting bath between them. Mom thought you might want your own rooms, but with this one, you can be together and still have your own space." He set the suitcases down. "I'll leave you to settle and will be back in about fifteen minutes to give Sarah the grand tour. That work for you?"

"Works for me," Sarah piped up. She grabbed her suitcase, the wheels leaving a trail on the plush burgundy carpet as she raced through the bathroom to the opposite room.

Jared faced Haley. "You and Sarah have nothing to be afraid of."

"I want to believe that," Haley said.

"Then believe it."

Her chin quivered. "Prove it."

"I intend to," he said, resisting the urge to touch her cheek. "You've done a wonderful job raising Sarah, Haley. She's a great kid."

"Sometimes she's seven going on twenty."

Jared watched Sarah investigate each corner of the room, then bounce on the bed and run her hand over the bedspread. "She wouldn't be who she is if she'd been raised any other way by any other person. You gave her that. Be confident in it."

"Sometimes love isn't enough," Haley murmured so softly he almost missed it.

Anger at Mitch pulsed through Jared, surprising him. So far, he'd laid most of the blame at Haley's feet. But Mitch was guilty, too. "Love is enough if it's the right kind," he said, shifting his gaze back to Haley. "Does this room work for you?"

Tears welled in her eyes.

"It works fine," she whispered. "Thank you."

"You're welcome." He tipped her chin and saw fragility reflecting in her eyes. Too many fears gripped her. He wanted to be the one to wipe away the mistrust and pain—the pain that Mitch had caused. He owed her that. "I'll see you at the barn in fifteen."

An hour later, they exited the chicken house on the final leg of the grand tour. Walt's Jeep pulled into the drive. Jared glanced at Sarah, but she was busy arguing the diet of molting chickens with Haley.

Neither had noticed the vehicle nor Walt's stunned look of disbelief as he gazed at Sarah's animated face.

For a moment Jared feared Walt would rush forward and frighten Sarah, but his mother's firm grip kept Walt grounded. Jared saw her lips move with one silent word.

Wait.

Sarah turned and looked up. A curious gleam lit her gray-green eyes. She smiled at Walt and waved.

Haley tensed. Before she turned around, she knew this was the moment she had dreaded.

"Is that him?" Sarah asked. "Is that my grandad?"

Haley placed a hand on Sarah's shoulder. "Yes." She couldn't meet Jared's eyes, but heard him move beside her in a protective gesture that she found oddly comforting. Walt walked toward them, his uncertain steps checked by Adele's more steady ones.

Sarah pressed close against Haley's leg. "What should I do?" she said. "What should I say?"

Haley bent close to Sarah's ear. "Don't be afraid to be yourself."

Sarah took a few steps forward. "Mom, I'm not scared, but what if he asks about my dad? I don't know anything. You never told me."

Sarah's accusation hit Haley like an arrow. "You never asked. You had me and Pop and Hap. I didn't think you needed anyone else."

"I didn't. But it's different now."

Haley rubbed the tight muscles along her neck. As if she needed to be reminded. Walt crossed the grass between the drive and the barn and stopped. Tears filled his eyes. He knelt to Sarah's level.

"Hello, Sarah. You look just like your dad."

Sarah didn't flinch. "Really?"

Walt nodded. "He would have loved to have known you."

Sarah cocked her head sideways. Her practical side overrode any uncertainty. "You think so? I never got to meet him." A heavy sigh escaped her lips.

Panic rose to Haley's throat. This was harder than she'd anticipated. She felt Jared's hand on her shoulder and pulled away. What did he think she was going to do, yank Sarah away and run or blurt out something awful about Mitch? She would never do that to Sarah. Walt and Sarah walked toward the house as Adele looked on.

"It'll be okay, Haley," Jared murmured.

"You don't know that," Haley said, watching Sarah laugh at something Walt said.

Sarah stopped and called back. "Mom, Grandad Walt is going to show me some pictures of my dad. Is that okay?" A worried look crept over her face. "I won't go if you don't want me to."

"You go ahead. I'll be in shortly."

Tears choked Haley's voice, but Sarah didn't seem to notice as she threw her arms around Walt and gave him the same impulsive hug she used to give Pop, then slipped her hand into his. Walt's feet seemed to float across the yard. Haley imagined Sarah's past memories emptying, being replaced with ones of her "new" family. She turned away from Adele's compassionate gaze.

"You're not losing a daughter, Haley," Adele said. "We hope you'll see this as gaining a family. I'll be in the house if you need anything."

Haley gulped in a breath. That Adele could be so generous after all that had transpired overwhelmed her. One look, one word from anyone right now and she would fall apart. She was losing pieces of herself and Sarah. She could sense it, feel it and was powerless to stop it.

"You and Sarah are safe here," Jared murmured.

Safe, maybe, as long as she kept the truth to herself. *The truth will set you free.* The truth was she wasn't safe at all. Haley gripped his arm, unaware of her fingernails pressing into his muscle until he flinched.

"I'm sorry." She patted the red marks and flushed. "I didn't mean to hurt you."

"You didn't. You couldn't."

She wasn't sure what he meant and didn't want to ask, but a flutter of wanting brushed against her heart. The staggering realization that she wanted this man in her life made her step back. She couldn't afford to care. He loved his brother. His faith was strong. Those two things created a huge chasm between them.

"I could hurt you, Jared. You have no idea."

His near black eyes seemed to grow darker. She squirmed. Jared faced her, his hands resting on her shoulders. She didn't have the energy to move away. Truth was she wanted his support—needed it—and hated herself for it. But maybe, until the shock of Sarah's acceptance of Walt wore off, she could lean on him just a little.

"Sarah said you were having bad dreams. I know being here has you spooked. How can I make it better?"

She pulled away. "You can't."

She couldn't tell him the truth. She cared what he thought. If he knew, he would look at her differently. She was tainted, used. Not by her own choice, but by the will of a man stronger than her and a God that had refused to hear her cry. What could she ever offer any man that Mitch hadn't already sullied?

Love. The word teased the corner of her mind. *You could love him. You could trust him with the truth.*

"Don't do this, Jared," she choked out. "Don't confuse me."

A smile tugged at his mouth. "I want you confused. Whatever Mitch did, I want you to see the opposite."

The breath left her body, leaving a crushing feeling in her chest. His eyes never left her face. She felt herself being pulled in two, as though someone had stretched her out on one of those medieval racks and her body had lost its give. She stepped back, breaking contact.

"I don't think that's possible," she said.

His gaze deepened. "Then you don't want it bad enough."

"How would you know? I'm here. I'm trying. You always get what you want, don't you?"

"Not always," he said, his look serious.

"Don't hurt us," she whispered. "I couldn't stand it if you hurt us." His genuine astonishment made her regret her words.

"Hurting you and Sarah is the furthest thing from my mind. I'm not so clouded by love for Mitch that I've forgotten what he was like before God changed him."

Haley broke eye contact and stepped back. A steel weight of fear pulled her away from him.

"Don't limit Sarah's capacity to love because you're afraid of it," he said.

Anger ripped along her spine. She lifted her gaze. "How would you know what I'm afraid of? Don't you dare judge me, Jared. Sarah's welfare is first. I'll allow her your version of Mitch's life, but don't ask me to sit around and listen to stories about a man I will always despise." Her voice rose a notch, unraveling that dark place in her mind. "I won't have her destroyed by things she doesn't need to know and wouldn't understand."

"Destroyed is a pretty strong word. You're hurting her and you don't even realize it. And what about you? You'll never have what you want as long as you're afraid. You don't show fear when you face the bulls. I don't understand why you choose to hide behind it now. Make me understand."

"You can't understand. You aren't a woman or a mother."

"Thank the good Lord for that. I like being a man, but it doesn't mean I don't feel any less," he said.

"If this is going to lead back to the forgiveness speech again, save your breath."

"What's forgiveness got to do with it? I thought we were talking about being afraid." Jared shook his head. "Regardless of what you believe, Mitch learned to give his fears to God and he learned the importance of forgiveness."

Haley's hands fisted. "And who did he forgive in the end, Jared? Me? For what?"

"I'm still trying to figure that out," he said, his eyes flashing like hot coal. "Mitch couldn't figure it out alone and neither can you or I."

Her breath burned in her throat. "Don't tell me what I have to do and stop trying to fix me." The hair along her neck tingled. "My life was just fine before you and your brother messed with it."

Hurt burned in his dark eyes.

She felt him shudder as he drew a deep breath.

"All right," he murmured, throwing up his hands. "You win. It doesn't really matter whether it's you or Mitch that needs to forgive or be forgiven, it doesn't change what is. It doesn't change your value, Haley. Someday you're going to realize you're worth fighting for, and you'll let go of all that misery you wrap around yourself like a winter blanket. Does it keep you warm or only make you realize how cold and empty your life really is?"

Chapter Nine

Walt and Sarah looked up from the great room table as Haley entered the front door. She caught a glimpse of Adele in the kitchen, then crossed the hardwood floor and stopped next to Sarah. Excitement radiated from her face.

"Look, Mom. Grandad Walt's right. I do look like my dad. How come you didn't tell me or have any pictures?"

Haley glanced at the photos on the mantel, the boxes of snapshots strung out across the coffee table. Pictures of an abundant life, minus the struggles and poverty she and Sarah had experienced.

Her gaze darted around the room and came to rest on Walt's hands draped over Sarah's shoulders, hugging her close to him, pulling her away from Haley and Hap and their old familiar way of life. Panic bubbled through her.

"Can you excuse us, Walt? We need to clean up."

"But Mom," Sarah protested.

"Now, Sarah."

Walt's gaze softened, pinning Haley to the spot near the stairs. "Go and do as your mom says. We'll have plenty of time to talk."

Sarah heaved a sigh. She sprinted across the room and up the stairs. Haley leveled her gaze on Walt. She didn't want to hurt this man, but she had to protect her daughter.

Protect Sarah or herself?

Both. Was there anything wrong in that?

"I want to thank you for bringing Sarah here," Walt said. "She's a gift. I know this has been hard for you." He shuffled uncomfortably. "Whatever happened before, we're here now. We're family. We can make things easier."

Easier? For whom? Haley couldn't have moved if she'd wanted to. Walt glanced at the floor, then back at her.

"I know it's probably too soon for me to say this, but Adele and I talked while you were gone. We would love it if you and Sarah would think about moving here."

"We have a life. In Colorado," Haley choked out. "We're just here for the next two weeks."

"Sarah's Mitch's daughter, too," Walt said.

She flinched. Did he think she would ever forget, especially when reminders of Mitch lingered at every turn? She shoved her arm out, palm forward. "Don't. Please don't put my daughter in a situation where she has to choose one of us over the other," she said, swallowing down rising panic. "I agreed to two weeks. Nothing more."

Walt's eyes softened. "I didn't mean to be hurtful. Sharing Sarah is new for you. I understand that. Take your time, Haley. We want this to work for all of us. In families everyone loses if everyone doesn't win." He offered a smile and a nod, then turned and went into the kitchen.

She heard him quietly talking to Adele and sank onto the bottom step. Walt's understanding and acceptance confused her far more than if he'd gotten angry and railed back.

"Mom," Sarah called from the stairs. "Come on."

Haley rose, the heaviness in her steps matched only by the heaviness in her heart. Sarah washed up and raced back down to find Walt. Hope of spending time with Sarah hit the ground.

During the next few days it seemed like Jared avoided her, but at dinner she'd find him studying her, an intensity in his brown eyes that both thrilled and terrified her. She wasn't immune to him any more than he was to her and his absence left a void she didn't understand.

Jared said she had value. That fear kept her looking back instead of ahead. He didn't know the consequences if she looked too far ahead and allowed herself to act on her dreams and hopes only to find she wasn't emotionally whole enough to sustain a relationship that might lead to something more serious.

She wasn't the only one who would be hurt if she tried and failed.

Sarah wanted a home and family—a father. Being here made that painfully clear. Haley's gut twisted. She wanted her soul to heal. She just didn't think it was possible in this house, with this family. She couldn't shatter the images of Mitch that Walt continued to share with Sarah, even though his memories were light years away from what she knew. Yet there had to be more for her own soul than emptiness and lost dreams.

Restlessness dogged her steps. She wandered out to the corral, saddled the three-year-old gelding Jared had asked her to work and led him to the round pen. She put the colt through some lead changes and side passes, then introduced him to a new movement. As always, he was quick to respond and eager to please. Grateful for the diversion, she let the horse's rhythm and the soft breeze carry her troubled thoughts away.

Jared set a piece of broken harness inside the barn and made a mental note to repair it later, then paused to watch the horse and rider move across the arena, their movements graceful and fluid. A whisper of admiration stirred his heart. Haley had a gift with horses that few people were given. He wished she recognized the value in it—and in herself. Had Mitch so crushed her that she didn't feel worthy of anything good?

She stopped the gelding and leaned over his neck, then scratched his ears and offered an affectionate hug. The animal bent his neck and nuzzled her boot.

Jared stood still, unwilling to break the moment. Her relaxed, easy manner transformed her face, making her radiant. He wanted to see that look on her face again. He wanted to be the reason for it. The thought stunned him. He missed a step, drawing the horse's attention. The moment was lost.

"I thought you'd be with Walt and Sarah," he said, trying to cover the lapse.

She dismounted and walked toward him, stopping at the fence. He got the feeling she felt safer for the barrier.

"I tried a few times, but they're so wrapped up in each other they hardly notice I'm around. I don't like being a third wheel."

"This is new for her, but she'll settle and come back to you. You're still the most important person in her life, Haley. She loves you."

"I know."

"Did Walt tell you that he'd like you and Sarah to stay longer?"

"More like indefinitely," she said. She ran the reins through her fingers. "How do you feel about that? It's your house."

"It's our home," he corrected. "It belongs to all of us. And yes. I'd like you to stay, too."

Her eyes challenged him. "I can't. I have to make my own way."

"Have you heard anything more?"

"You're referring to the investigation," he said.

"I am."

Brave words. Frightened words. Jared's chest tightened, but he held her gaze. "I told you, Haley. It's out of my hands now. I'm sorry. We'll both have to wait."

She rubbed one hand against her jeans, then gripped the reins so hard her knuckles turned white. She opened the gate and led the horse out of the round pen. She didn't like being pushed. Neither did he.

"I want things to be the way they were before Mitch walked into that arena and you found me."

"You can't go back, Haley. Neither of us can."

Her shoulders drooped a fraction, but her head remained high. "Fix what you took away," she murmured. "Give me back my life, Jared."

Her plea knifed through him. "Your life is tied to ours now. Through Sarah. That isn't something either of us can change," he said, drinking in the sheen of her golden hair. Unshed tears made her eyes sparkle like amethyst stones. "I don't want it to change."

Her chin quivered. He reached for her hand, but she pulled away and hurried to the barn, her back as rigid as a fence post. She slammed the door behind her. It creaked open. He saw her slumped against the horse, her shoulders shaking with sobs she refused to utter.

His chest squeezed. It was as though God had taken her pain and placed it on him. The need to comfort her welled inside him, but she wouldn't welcome him. Maybe not ever. He went to his office, closed the door and sat down.

Heavenly Father. The prayer lumped in his throat.

He stopped, then rested his elbows on the desk and put his face in his hands. He'd been so impulsive. He'd left God out of his decision to request an investigation, and everything since then had had a domino effect, each fallen piece landing directly on Haley. He'd been unfair and selfish.

His mind raced with memories, foremost all the things Haley hadn't said about Mitch, but all the things her mannerisms did say. Silent rage at his brother nearly unraveled his control. He'd told Haley she couldn't face her fear alone. Well, ditto. He couldn't face his fear about Mitch alone either. He swallowed, then fisted his hands under his chin.

Lord God. I'm not sure I can forgive Mitch, let alone expect Haley to. I care about her, Lord, and she refuses to let You into her life. Help her find her way back to You. And help me forgive Mitch and find a way to help Haley forgive him, too. In Jesus's name.

Sunday morning, Haley put the last ribbon in Sarah's long black hair. "You look lovely," she said. "Have fun at church."

"You should go, Mom. It's rude to not go when someone asks you, especially if you're staying at their house."

"And it's rude to speak to your mother in that voice, too. I taught you better manners," Haley said, meeting Sarah's gaze in the mirror.

"Going won't hurt. It's only once." Sarah turned around, her gray-green eyes wide and beseeching. "It would make me and Grandad Walt so happy. Even Uncle Jared said he'd love for you to come."

Haley stiffened.

"Pleeeezzze." Sarah ran to Haley's closet and pulled out a lavender blouse and white jeans. "You don't have to wear a dress. Hap says God doesn't care how you come. He just wants you to come."

Haley dropped her gaze. Shamed by a seven-year-old. Hap had always been there to smooth over the church issue, but he wasn't here. Even if he were, Haley knew what he'd say. "'Bout time ya faced yer issues with yer Maker, girl." Problem was, those issues were so monumental that if she were inclined, she didn't know how or even where to begin.

Sarah rummaged through her suitcase and pulled out Haley's amethyst earrings. "I brought these. Hap says a girl just never knows." She cocked her head sideways. "What did he mean?"

"Someday I'll tell you," Haley said, her voice too choked to say more. She ran her fingers over the earrings, remembering the day she'd admired them in a gift shop in Calgary. After seeing the price, she promptly put them back. These were Pop's last gift to her and she knew the sacrifice he'd made to buy them.

"Sarah," Adele called from downstairs. "We're going to be late if you don't come on."

"Please, Mom. Come. We'll wait."

Haley pushed her hair back. Going might make her feel closer to Pop. Right now, she needed that.

"All right. Give me five minutes," Haley said, already regretting the impulse.

Sarah hugged her tight and skipped down the hall.

Walt and Adele looked surprised and pleased when Haley hurried downstairs. Sarah's huge smile lifted the heaviness in her heart, but it was Jared's response that held her captive.

He wouldn't take his eyes off her and the light in their dark depths stirred something inside her she thought would never live again.

"I'm glad you're coming," he said, clearing his throat.

Twenty minutes later they arrived at a small white country church much like the ones she and Pop had attended throughout her childhood years. Memories played like an old movie through Haley's mind. There was a time she'd blindly trusted God. Why did He abandon her? She hesitated at the door and felt Jared stop behind her.

"You can sit out here if you're too uncomfortable. I'll stay, too."

Haley shook her head. "I have to do this. It's important to Sarah."

"Don't do it for Sarah," he said, his voice inches from her ear. "Do it because it's important for you."

She felt the love inside as soon as she stepped through the door. Jared introduced her to several people. As the service began, she was surprised to hear his deep baritone voice lift in song. She closed her eyes and listened, trying not to be so aware of his arm brushing against her shoulder.

She was determined to not listen to the minister's sermon, but the title intrigued her from the start and when he spoke about faith that stands the test, the words rooted in her heart. What was wrong with her that her faith floundered when others remained strong regardless of their circumstances? Why was she different, and why did it matter?

All the way home, Sarah chattered about the new friends she'd made. Haley sat quietly in the backseat with Adele and Sarah, catching Jared's eye every so often in the mirror. Heaviness weighted her heart again. Going today was a huge mistake. Church was one more reason she couldn't stay here. If people knew…if Jared knew.

As soon as Jared shut the engine off, Haley pleaded a headache and went to her room. She phoned Hap, just to hear his voice and be closer to the one place she felt safe, but peace eluded her. Hap signed off with "I love you, Haley"—something she always knew but he never said. He was worried, and she'd done nothing to relieve him of that burden. If she tried talking to God again, would He hear her or just drop another bomb like every other time she'd taken the plunge?

"God," she whispered. "I trusted You once. Now it's broken and I can't fix it. I just can't."

It is better to take refuge in the Lord than to trust in man.

The verse came out of nowhere, echoing in her mind like a call in the canyon. She ached with an inner pain. She had disobeyed Pop and trusted Mitch and in that disobedience, she tied God's hands with her choice. Was it fair to completely blame God? Hap said God wouldn't go against a person's will to choose. Did that mean she must live with the consequences of her choice to disobey Pop and go with Mitch? She'd been so young, so trusting.

"Why, God? I just need to know why."

She waited for something else to pop into her head, a verse, a voice, anything to assure her God was there, but nothing happened. He was gone, and she was alone.

The next morning Haley stopped outside the kitchen and listened to the sound of Sarah's laughter. She stepped into the room. Walt, Sarah and Adele hovered around the stove, steam rising from a pot hidden from view. Canning jars stood upside down on the counter. The kitchen was littered with colanders, boxes of pectin and sugar. A huge basket filled with end-of-season peaches sat on the floor.

Sarah looked up and smiled. "Hey, Mom. How's the head?"

"Doable."

"Good morning, Haley," Adele said. "Coffee's on and there are eggs in the microwave if you're hungry." Walt pulled a cup off the shelf, filled it with steaming coffee and handed it to Haley.

"Thank you," she said, her gaze darting around the kitchen. Jared was nowhere to be seen. Some of the morning brightness evaporated. She lifted the cup to her lips, hiding her disappointment behind the rising steam cloud.

"It's supposed to be jelly," Sarah said, lifting the spoon from the pot. "You promised to help, remember?"

"Must have been a brain lapse," Haley said, her thoughts turning to the last time she, Pop and Sarah had hovered over a boiling pot of Colorado peaches. "It doesn't look like jelly," she said. "So what are we making?"

Walt smiled and Haley realized she'd referred to them as a unit for the first time. We. Heat crept up her neck.

"We are making peach butter," Walt said, mashing more peaches in the colander, then removing the skin and seed.

"Let me stir those in," Sarah said, turning back to the stove. "This is going to be so good. We haven't done this since Poppy died."

Haley stared into the mug, then blinked back a tear.

"Sarah's been telling us about your dad," Adele said. "He sounds like a very unique person."

"He was one of a kind," Haley said.

Adele handed Sarah a bigger spoon and began measuring sugar. "I'd love to hear more about him sometime." She dumped the sugar into the pot and instructed Sarah on the importance of not letting the bottom scorch.

A surge of envy ripped through Haley. She should be doing this with Sarah. How could they ever go back to the way it used to be? She could never give Sarah the things that Mitch's family offered.

"You best eat, Haley," Adele said. "I'm afraid Jared got a little carried away with the peach buying. There're two more bushels on the porch."

Tears stung Haley's throat. She stepped into the mudroom to collect herself. This scene mirrored the one when Pop was alive, but the situation and the people were different. No matter how many memories it stirred or how much it hurt, she had to see this through. For Sarah—and like Jared had said—for herself, too.

Someone behind her slipped a bib apron around her neck. Haley jumped and scrambled to steady the mug, then felt two arms slip around her waist. A gentle tug on the apron strings pulled her backwards. She landed against a rock hard chest and tried to bolt sideways, but the pressure held.

"Family efforts require all hands. Can't have you getting your clothes all messed up with peach juice," Jared said. He stepped back, letting a rush of morning air settle between them, then tied the strings.

"There's something wrong with this picture of you and me in aprons," Haley said, wishing her awareness of him didn't make her so jumpy.

"Another news flash. I can cook," he murmured, his breath fanning her hair.

She kept her back to him, wanting him to pull her

into his arms, but he didn't. That was just one more pipe dream, close yet unattainable. She wanted to belong here with Jared, but by the end of the week she and Sarah would be safely back in Colorado, and he would become just another memory—a pleasant one for the most part, but a memory just the same. It had been a long time since she'd allowed herself the luxury of a pleasant dream. Even a temporary one. What harm would a little dreaming do?

"I'm glad you're feeling better," he said, stepping closer. His chest nearly touched her back as he adjusted her shirt collar over the bib strap. "I missed you."

The urge to lean against him overruled her instinct to move away. A flash of the fear that always kept her on the fringe of happiness ripped through her—God dangling the carrot in front of the horse only to pull it away. He'd helped create the problems in her by shaping the events in her life. Why wouldn't He remove the fear?

Why hadn't she asked?

The question hammered against her heart. She stiffened her back and felt Jared's amused chuckle. She wouldn't be toyed with, yet she had the distinct feeling neither God nor Jared were playing games. Both wanted something she couldn't deliver. They stepped into the kitchen together. Adele, Walt and Sarah seemed oblivious to the tension, but she knew Jared felt it, even seemed to find her discomfiture amusing.

"Welcome back to the land of the living, Haley," he murmured.

"What do you mean by that?" she asked.

"I think you know." He pulled her heavy hair back and fastened it with a piece of string. Walt and Adele glanced their way, smiled and returned to their tasks. "You're a stubborn woman, Haley Clayton."

"I have to be. Remember, I make my living in a man's world."

"I can't argue with that. I think we'd better pitch in and help before I give in to the urge to kiss more than your forehead," he whispered.

She stepped away and glanced at him, certain he was jesting, but the tenderness in his expression knocked the air from her lungs and threw her off balance. He moved around her and joined Walt, who was slicing more peaches near the sink. What would it be like to be loved by a man like Jared Sinclair? What would it be like to love him back?

"Come on, Mom," Sarah said. "If you don't help, we'll be here all day. Grandad Walt said if we got done in time, we could go down to the pond and swim."

"Okay, what do you want me to do?" Haley asked, glancing at Adele. Light banter sidelined Haley's doubts, at least for now. But she knew they'd come back in full force when she least expected it. She wanted to go on living this dream, but nothing good would come of riding a fine line between what reality was and what she wanted reality to be.

"You and Jared wash, slice and pit," Adele said. "Then pass them on to Walt to mash. Sarah and I will do the rest. With any luck we'll be finished before supper."

Jared tossed Haley a peach pit. "Come on, partner. We're behind. The rest of the crew is waiting on us." He offered a dazzling smile that made her heart jump. "I promise to be good."

For the next several hours, the kitchen filled with laughter. A warm camaraderie that Haley hadn't felt for a long time kept even Mitch's shadow at bay. It was good to smile, to feel part of a family again. She craved to belong to something, to someone, to be complete and happy without her secret threatening her happiness.

"You have wrinkles in your forehead," Jared said.

"That will win you points," Haley replied.

"I said the wrong thing."

"Men usually do," she said.

"Is it something I did?"

She shook her head. "I was just thinking." She grabbed another peach and concentrated on slicing out the pit.

"There's a Dutch oven cooking contest over at the dude ranch tomorrow night," Adele said. "You and Haley should go, Jared."

"Wow. A date," Sarah piped up, her eyes lighting with mischief. "Mom never goes on dates."

"Really?" Jared said, sliding a sideways look at Haley. His eyes darkened. "Then we'll have to do something about that, won't we? Will you do me the honor of escorting me so we can show the 'dudes' how real western cooking is done?"

"Mom can't cook," Sarah said, sniffing the boiling peach pot.

"You're kidding," Jared said. "She grew up on a ranch and can't cook?"

Sarah shrugged. "Hap tried to teach her, but he said every time he eats something she's made he has to stock up on antacids."

"Out of the mouth of babes," Walt chuckled.

A flush crept up Haley's neck. She shot Sarah a warning look. "Is everyone done having fun at my expense? I didn't exactly have time to learn. I was too busy keeping our heads above water," she said, hating the defensive ring in her voice.

The room grew quiet. Haley pressed her hands against the counter and dropped her head.

Jared faced her, forcing her to look up. "I'm sorry things have been so rough for you and Sarah. It's time you had a little fun. I can use a Dutch oven. I even have a few tricks for making the job easier. Would you like me to teach you?"

Haley couldn't breathe. She locked gazes with Jared and couldn't pull away. The warmth of his shoulder against hers, the scent of his aftershave, the tilt of amusement on his lips that lit a twinkle in his eyes filled the empty space in heart. The moment lasted an eternity and sizzled with a connection she didn't want to end yet feared to continue.

"You have a peach peeling on your nose," Jared said softly. He plucked the fruit from her skin with a touch so light she thought she'd imagined it. "Will you go with me? I promise to bring Rolaids and not make any comments about charred biscuits."

"Better take some Alka-Seltzer, too," Sarah piped up, drawing a laugh from Walt and Adele. It pulled Haley back from the space where, for just a few seconds, only she and Jared had occupied. Sarah seemed oblivious, but the moment hadn't gone unnoticed by Walt and Adele. Adele's worried look offset Walt's pleasured smile.

"Come with me," Jared persisted.

Haley threw up her hands. "Do I have a choice?"

"With me, you always have a choice, Haley. Don't ever forget that."

Her heart lurched. Being with Jared, sharing the things that made him laugh, was what she wanted. Even if nothing could come of it, she'd have something pleasant to think back on when she left here.

"All right," she said, dropping her gaze. "I'll go."

Sarah climbed down from the chair, gave Jared a high five and hugged Haley. "Way to go, Mom. You've got a date. It's about time."

Haley was too mortified to look at anyone.

"You don't think she'll back out, do you?" Jared asked, addressing Sarah.

"She better not."

"Promise," Jared said, lifting Haley's chin with his finger, "you won't back out."

She hesitated a second. "I won't back out."

By the time they'd finished the peaches and cleaned up, it was too late to swim. Haley had worked herself into emotional exhaustion weighing the pros and cons of her upcoming "date." Whatever had possessed her to agree? She pleaded a return of her headache and hurried Sarah off to bed.

Seconds after Sarah's head hit the pillow, she was sound asleep. Haley watched the girl's chest rise and fall with each breath. She fingered a silky strand of Sarah's dark hair, then Sarah's eyelid cracked open.

"I love you, Mom," she murmured, opening the other eyelid. "Uncle Jared likes you a lot. I hope we can stay here longer."

Haley's chest squeezed. "Don't you want to go home? Home to Hap, and Spinner and our old life?" Mitch's picture mocked her from Sarah's bed stand. Haley resisted the urge to throw it against the wall. She tucked the sheet around Sarah.

"Hap would come here if you asked him," Sarah said yawning and burrowing deeper into the pillow. "We belong here. Grandad Walt said so."

She bent and kissed Sarah's cheek. "We'll talk about it later. Get some sleep. I love you," she whispered, but Sarah's eyes had already closed. Haley slumped in the chair and spent a restless night watching her daughter sleep, more uncertain about their future than ever.

Chapter Ten

The next day passed far too quickly for Haley. It was nearly five when Sarah skipped into the barn.

"Come on, Mom." She wrinkled her nose and flicked a piece of manure off Haley's shirt. "Uncle Jared's been inside for the last half hour getting stuff ready. You've gotta take a bath and start getting ready." Sarah pulled her toward the house.

Haley dragged her feet. What had possessed her to agree to this? If she could make it to the weekend, her two-week obligation would be finished. She and Sarah could go home and hopefully get back to their lives. She rammed the pitchfork into the hay and headed for the house. Who was she kidding? Nothing would be the same again. She'd still have to share Sarah, though not quite as much.

A few hours later, Jared placed a large Dutch oven filled with cowboy stew and topped with biscuits into the back of his SUV. He ushered Haley into the front seat. She could still find an excuse to back out. She fidgeted with the seatbelt and refused to look at him.

Jared hadn't been able to take his eyes off her from the minute she'd walked down the stairs. Her golden hair hung in loose waves to her waist, fastened to one side with a comb of German silver hearts that matched the belt around her slender waist. Lavender accents on her white blouse deepened her eyes. The familiar scent of honeysuckle filled the vehicle. Underneath her nervousness, he sensed a hint of reserved excitement. It wasn't all he'd hoped for, but it was a start.

"You look beautiful tonight," he said.

"Thank you. You look pretty nice yourself," she stammered.

"Just nice? I spent hours getting ready," he said, grinning.

Her tense smile relaxed. "You did good. Sarah's impressed."

He chanced a quick look at her profile. "Sarah's not the one I want to impress."

She clasped her hands in her lap and pressed herself into the seat. Thirty minutes later they pulled up at Martin Davis's dude ranch. The double barn doors stood open. Straw bales and ropes outlined a huge wooden platform where dozens of couples were already tapping their toes in time with the music and taking advantage of the games Martin had placed at tables around the room.

A dessert table stood in the corner with a huge

punch bowl in the middle. Japanese lanterns lit the interior with an intimate glow. Opposite the barn, a trench of hot coals sent steam rising from assorted pots hanging from hooks.

Jared lifted his pot from the car. He greeted several people and introduced Haley to a few, conscious of the speculative glances following them as he led her to the cooking pits. Let them speculate that he'd finally been caught. He glanced at Haley, finding the prospect appealing. If only he knew where she stood with her faith.

Haley crowded close behind him. "I don't think I can do this, Jared. I'll burn everything and embarrass you in front of all these people."

"That'll never happen. I'll talk you through it. The contest requires one of us prepare the dish, which I've done, and the other to cook it. That's your job."

"You should have let me do the prep work."

"Your fault. You were hiding," he said. "Just follow my instructions and you'll be fine." He grasped her hand and headed for the entry table, took his number then pointed to a vacant spot near the fire pit. "Come on. There's no way you can mess this up."

Haley laughed. "Obviously you weren't listening when Sarah tried to warn you. I can't cook over a stove. What makes you think I can do it over a campfire?"

He bowed slightly. "The difference is I'm here to help you. Together we can do anything." He hadn't thought about his impulsive quest for justice in a long time. There was definitely value in allowing God to use him instead of following his own agenda.

A flush crept into Haley's's cheeks that he suspected had nothing to do with the heat from the pits. She was downright gorgeous when her eyes weren't shaded with doubt and fear. One more step toward the healing process he'd prayed for. Tonight her eyes sparkled, and he'd made it happen. His heart was full.

"What do I do?" she whispered.

"Hang the pot over that medium hook, leave it for twenty minutes, then come back and put one scoop of hot coals on the top of the pot and cook it for another ten or until the biscuits are brown on top."

Her eyes widened. "That's it?"

"That's it." Jared smiled back.

"What do we do in the meantime?"

"I play a mean game of checkers. Wanna give it a go?"

"You bet," she laughed. "I play an even meaner game. But better set your watch so I know when to come back and stir the pot."

Lively country music greeted them as they headed for the tables. For the next few minutes, Jared watched her concentrate on beating him, then his watch alarm sounded.

"You're a tough competitor," he said. "I knew it that day I saw you on the barrels."

Haley grew quiet. Jared could have kicked himself for the reminder. Truth was, he remembered every moment in her presence, the good and the bad. They headed back to the cooking pits. Haley scooped coals onto the Dutch oven lid and glanced at him.

"That enough?"

"It'll do."

"Ten minutes more?" she asked.

"More or less. All we have to do is brown the biscuit tops." Jared took her hand and led her to a table. "We'd better stay close."

"Where did you learn all this?" she asked.

"Mom. She's a remarkable woman. There were times before she met Walt that a pot of stew was all we had for a week."

Quiet settled between them. Several times, Jared caught her watching him, curiosity in her eyes. Several minutes later, Haley checked the biscuits, then removed the pot and set it on the judging table. The quick-paced music echoing from the loft ended. A slow tune blared over the speaker.

"We've got some time before the judging starts. Walk with me," Jared said, leading her toward the rear door.

"I don't think…" she hedged.

"My intentions are honorable, I promise. You can't come to Martin's place and not see this view of the Black Hills on a moonlit night. You're safe with me, Haley."

Her doubt pricked him like a thorn. He led her out back, stopping near the corrals. She lifted her gaze to the sky, the light dancing off her hair and shimmering off her face like snow crystals.

"You're right. It's incredible," she murmured, placing her hands on the fence rail. The music shifted and the distinct sound of Patsy Cline's "Crazy" echoed through the night. He moved behind her and touched her shoulders, felt her resistance even though she didn't pull away. He closed his eyes and rested his face against her ear, murmuring the words along with the vocalist.

The tremor racing through her body touched him. Right now, this minute, her past with Mitch was unimportant. He was a man, and, God willing, she was the woman he wanted in his life. He brushed his face against hers and heard her breath catch. Jared wanted the moment to last forever. He murmured the next phrase.

Haley turned into his arms. She was powerless to draw away. Didn't want to. Whatever lay ahead, she would have this moment, steal it, cherish it, hold it close, because all too soon, it would be gone. She'd be alone again. Jared's lips nuzzled her temple. She held tightly to his arm, afraid if she let go, her weakened limbs would collapse.

I'm falling in love with you, Jared. The silent admission didn't generate fear, only a sadness that what she'd finally found she could never have. The vocalist began the last round of the song. Jared whispered along with her.

Haley's velvet skin invited his touch. Her heart pounded against his. He spanned her waist with his hands, drawing her close, then dipped his head and claimed her lips. It was the sweetest thing he'd ever experienced. When he broke away, the look of wonder on her face made him smile.

"I don't want you and Sarah to leave." Haley's shallow breathing stopped for the space of a heartbeat. Tucking his chin, he looked into her beautiful eyes. "Say you'll stay."

Her eyes closed and opened again. This couldn't be real. Good things like Jared couldn't happen to her. Walt's words echoed through her mind. *Jared's always fixed Mitch's mistakes.* Adele had said the same thing. Even Jared had voiced something to that effect. She was a mistake that Jared needed to fix because he loved Mitch, not her. She looked into his eyes, wanting desperately to believe what she saw in their depths, then shook her head.

"I can't."

The strains of the music faded as the vocalist finished the last lyric. Jared's shoulders slumped a little. He stood motionless in the moonlight, his dark eyes shimmering with disappointment. Another lively tune began. The moment was lost. He took her hand and led her back toward the refreshment table.

"It was a mistake coming here," she said, not meeting his eyes. "Would you please take me home?"

"Which home, Haley?"

Confusion clouded her face then a slow blush pinked her cheeks. "Take me back to the house. Please."

"Is that what you really want?"

"Yes."

One look at her face told him it wasn't. Sadness shadowed her eyes. Whatever damage Mitch had done, he'd done well. It was too late now for a lot of things. Emptiness hollowed the place in his heart where hope had sprung. He spoke to the woman behind the entry table, then led Haley to the car.

"We can stay long enough to find out who's won if you want," she said, staring at the ground.

He already knew who had won, and it had nothing to do with the cooking contest. "Maddie's got it covered," he said. "Haley, I would never hurt you."

Her eyes clouded. "You already have."

She slid into the seat. The drive home was silent. She exited the car and ran into the house before he had turned the engine off, leaving him with the feeling that he'd just lost the most precious thing to come into his life.

Morning came too soon to suit Haley. She splashed water onto her face, then pressed her fingers into her temples. Sarah slipped into the bathroom and closed the door.

"Mom, some cows broke through the fence. Uncle Jared needs us to help him. Grandma and Grandpa left already."

Haley moaned, slid a washcloth under the water, then wrung it out and put it over her eyes. "They're gone? Where?"

"Don't you remember?" Sarah huffed. "They're helping with the bake sale at church today. They're supposed to come back and get me later." She grabbed her hat off the bed. "Come on. We need to help."

Haley looked into the mirror. Her pale reflection stared back. She couldn't face Jared after last night. And especially not after her own awareness of how important he'd become to her. She straightened and turned away from the reflection.

Sarah's face scrunched. "What's wrong?"

"I don't think I can help. My head is spinning."

Sarah looked doubtful. "You're mad at Uncle Jared, aren't you? That's why you came home early last night. Uncle Jared told Grandma we weren't staying. Is that true?" Her voice rose a notch.

Haley's heart twisted. She'd hoped to break the news a little more gently. "Were you listening at doors again?"

Sarah shrugged and dropped her gaze. "How else am I supposed to find out what's going on? Why are you mad at Uncle Jared?"

"I'm not mad at Jared." Haley bent to Sarah's level. *How do I make her see?* She took a deep breath and pressed her fingers against her temples. "There are some things you won't understand until you grow up, Sarah. You knew this visit was temporary. It is what it is. A visit. Not a move. This isn't our home. It isn't our life."

Tears filled Sarah's eyes, spilling down her cheeks. "But it could be. You, Hap and me, we could be happy here. And Uncle Jared wants you here. I know he does. You won't come. I heard him say so.

If this was my dad's home, doesn't that make it mine, too? Grandad Walt said so."

Walt. With all his good intentions, he wasn't above manipulation after all. Haley gathered Sarah close, savoring the feel of her daughter's warmth and cursing the abnormal childhood that had made her as comfortable in an adult world as one made up of her own peers.

Walt wouldn't have to threaten to take Sarah. She'd willingly stay if Haley gave the word. And maybe even if she didn't. All of her worst fears were becoming reality.

"Why can't we stay?" Sarah cried. "It's not like my dad was a bad person because he couldn't take care of us. I want to be where he was and know about him." Sarah's shoulder's shook. Her bottom lip quivered. She sucked it into her mouth.

Oh, God. His name was a mere thought in Haley's mind, a silent plea on her lips. A sense of His presence surrounded her, something she hadn't felt or allowed herself to feel for a very long time. The lump in her throat grew too large to swallow, the tears behind her eyes impossible to stay. She let them roll down her face and tightened her grip around her sobbing child.

"We can't stay, Sarah. It's a grown-up thing that I can't explain to you right now, but someday I will. Besides, Hap needs us and you have school soon, and your friends…"

"I can change schools. This is our family, Mom. The only one we have. You're going to ruin it because you're scared of Uncle Jared." She released her hold on Haley's neck and pushed away.

"Where did you get that notion?" Haley said.

"I may be a kid, but I'm not dumb. He likes you a lot. I think you like him, too, but you're scared to be around him. It's silly to be afraid of boys, but that's why you made him bring you home, isn't it?"

"That's not true, Sarah. I'm not afraid, and I do like Jared."

Far too much.

"You were crying last night," Sarah said, her gaze challenging. "I heard you."

Haley's chest tightened. "I'm sorry. I never meant for you to hear. Leaving here is about you and me taking care of ourselves, making our own way. It doesn't mean you can't come back and visit. I would never take that away from you or your grandparents."

"But I want to *stay,* always," Sarah pleaded.

Haley stifled her agitation. This was what she'd feared all along. Now it was actually happening. Now she had to do the one thing she'd vowed never to do. Hurt her child. Loving Jared was just an added complication she hadn't counted on, but would deal with, later.

"Sarah, the hardest part about growing up is learning that we can't always have and do the things we want."

"You go home and come and get me when it's time for school."

Haley's patience snapped. She rose and leaned against the sink. "No. I can't keep going back and forth. I have to find work, and that may not be easy right now. We're leaving Saturday. I don't want to hear any argument about it."

Sarah's lips quivered, but her chin lifted. She stomped to the door. "Okay, but I don't have to like it," she said. "I'll tell Uncle Jared you can't help. We'll get the cows ourselves." She banged the door behind her.

Haley winced, then followed. "Sarah. Wait." Sarah paused at the top of the stairs but didn't turn around. "You know I love you. I only want the very best for you."

"That would be staying here," she said half-turning.

Haley rested her head on the door jamb, too weary to argue. "I love you, too," Sarah said, dropping her gaze.

"Tell Jared I'll come."

"Okay," Sarah said, brushing tears away. "You're not going to change your mind about leaving, are you?"

Haley shook her head. "No."

"I can keep hoping 'til Saturday, can't I?"

"You can hope," Haley said, feeling her daughter's hurt, "but my decision stands. I'll be down in a minute."

Sarah disappeared down the stairs. Haley closed the door. A knot of fear rose to her throat. Sarah was thriving here. What child wouldn't with a loving set of grandparents, a doting uncle, a mother close by and unbiased memories of a father she wanted to believe in?

She pulled a light jacket from her suitcase, catching

her finger in the zipper, welcoming the physical pain. Leaving was in her and Sarah's best interest.

Jared's face formed in her mind, then the image disappeared and she saw Mitch, as clearly as if his physical presence stood before her. Nausea rose to her throat. She closed her mind, forcing back the memory of what followed. She and Sarah had to get home, back to Hap and the life they knew. Back on safe ground. She raced for the barn, the sun beating on her head, memories of Mitch nipping at her heels.

Jared led the horses from the corral as Haley stormed off the porch. Something had sent her over the edge. He sensed it in the way she moved, the way she glanced behind her as though something or someone followed.

His pulse accelerated. She's running again. *Help me understand what she needs, Lord.* Leaving things in God's hands was proving harder than he'd thought, but it's what he should have done in the first place instead of trying to take matters into his own hands.

Haley pulled her hair up and tucked it under her hat. Sarah exited the barn, leading a smaller horse behind her. She glanced at Haley and frowned, then gripped the saddle strings and pulled herself onto the horse's back.

"Thanks for coming," Jared said. "Sarah said you didn't feel well. You don't have to do this."

"You can't do it alone," she said, not meeting his gaze.

"I could," he said. "It would just take a lot longer."

Haley accepted the reins. Their fingers touched, and she pulled away. "I'll be okay."

"Suppose you will if stubbornness has anything to do with it," Jared said, hoping for a smile that never appeared. "How about Sarah? Is she comfortable doing this?"

Haley nodded. "Hap and Pop ran cattle. She's been on horses since before she could walk."

"Good. The cows aren't too scattered, so it shouldn't take long. Once I get them started toward the main gate, Sarah can bring up the rear and push them forward, not too fast, though, or they'll scatter into the brush. Haley, keep them between you and the fence and follow the fence line to the gate."

"We know what to do, Jared," Haley said, mounting her horse. "Just show us where you want them to end up."

Jared checked his cinch and joined Haley and Sarah. "We've got a twenty-minute ride before I can do that. Any questions?"

Sarah and Haley shook their heads. Side by side, they rode down the road toward the hills beyond the house. Minutes later, they entered the tree-lined ridge bordering public grazing lands. Haley gazed across a land uncluttered by fence posts and barbed wire. Her thoughts centered on the beauty and freedom of place and time. All the troubles of the past few days evaporated into the landscape.

Scattered cattle grazed in the distance, looking much like dots on a page. The scent of pine and sage filled the air. She shook her rope loose and coiled it again, then glanced at Jared and Sarah riding a comfortable distance ahead. Jared sat tall in the saddle, confident and disturbingly handsome. Sarah chattered comfortably at his side, small and innocent and totally trusting. This felt right. But feelings were deceptive and untrustworthy. Still, how could she take Sarah from a life that she seemed born to live?

Jared broke off and pointed at Sarah to head down the draw. "Wait there," he called. "Once I've got them going, keep a good distance so you don't rush them." Sarah turned her horse around. "You sure you're up for this?" Jared asked.

"Yup." Sarah smiled for the first time today.

"Good girl," Jared grinned back.

Haley guarded her heart. She was proud of Sarah's capabilities at so young an age. Proud, too that Jared recognized them and wasn't afraid to utilize them. But it hurt to feel the closeness between Jared and Sarah and be the outsider looking in. *You don't have to be outside. You could let him in.*

Or not. Haley rested her arms across the saddle horn. She wouldn't add to the day's difficulties. Her fingers tightened around the reins.

Jared smiled. Haley's chest tightened.

"I'll drive them towards that tree grove," he said. "There's an orange gate about two miles down. You can't see it from here, but that's where they need to go. Just head toward those rock formations and go a little to the left."

Haley nodded and moved behind a line of trees until the cattle came in sight, then closed in to guide them along the fence. Jared kicked his horse into a gallop and flushed four heifers from the brush. He moved with grace and speed. It was obvious he belonged to the land and the life. Haley tucked the scene into her memory, then concentrated on the cattle.

By the time they reached the gate, the sun was high in the sky. Haley rode ahead. Jared herded the last of the cattle from the trees and pushed them toward open range. Leaning over, she reached for the gate latch, but it held firm. The cattle drew closer. Haley dismounted and leaned her shoulder into the rusty spring, then pulled the gate wide and re-mounted. The cattle passed through, bawling loudly and kicking up a dust cloud.

"We make a good team," Jared said, closing the gate and brushing a sleeve across his sweaty brow.

"Wow," Sarah said. "That was so fun. We haven't done that since Hap quit running cattle last year. Can we do it again?"

"Maybe," Jared said, turning his horse around. "I'm glad you had fun. How's the headache?" he asked, addressing Haley.

"Fine." In truth it was pounding, but the atmosphere was so relaxed she didn't want to break the spell.

"We'd better head back," Jared said. "I did a temporary fix on the fence earlier, but I'll need to come back and do it right."

"Is it okay if I ride ahead?" Sarah asked, looking

at Jared. "Grandma was coming back to take me to the bake sale at church."

"That's up to your mom," Jared said.

Haley nodded. She didn't want to be alone with him, but she didn't need another excuse for Sarah to be angry with her. "You sure you know the way?"

"Yup. Go through the third gate, catch the road and look for the barn."

Haley waved Sarah on. She kicked the horse into a gallop and rode ahead. Haley fell into an easy jog beside Jared.

"I take it you haven't reconsidered," Jared said.

Haley shook her head. They veered off the main trail and headed down a gulch. This wasn't the way back. She stopped the horse.

Jared circled back. "There's something I want you to see," he said.

They followed the gulch, exiting into a huge open valley. Charred trees pointed to the sky, others lay in burnt clumps across the lush valley floor littered with wildflowers. A gentle breeze tickled her cheek and the piercing cry of a hawk echoed across the blue sky.

"It's beautiful," Haley said. "So peaceful."

"It wasn't a few years ago. It's easy to forget the beauty when you witness the devastation of a fire. You think the land will never recover."

She stood in the stirrups and shaded her eyes.

"It's more beautiful now than before," Jared said. "Kind of symbolic, isn't it?"

"What do you mean?"

"You've been through a wildfire, too, Haley, and like this canyon, you've come back, stronger and lovelier."

She sat back down, tears welling in her eyes. "You didn't know me before."

"I know you now. Beauty comes from ashes. Like you and Sarah. You deserve to be happy. Don't convince yourself you don't."

The hawk's shadow passed over them again. Haley wished she could latch on to the tail and for a little while, soar above her problems and feel free. The sympathy in Jared's eyes was more than she could stand—one more reason not to stay. She loved him. She could handle his anger, even his pain and blaming her for Mitch's loss, but never his pity.

"We'd better get back," she said, turning the horse around.

Jared followed. "Someday, you have to stop running," he murmured.

His words followed Haley all the way to the main road.

"I need…" both began together and stopped.

"You go first," Jared said.

Haley lifted a rein, cuing the horse to pick up his pace. "I need you to know how much I appreciate your hospitality."

"But…" Jared said, looking straight ahead. "You're still leaving."

"We have to get back to our lives, Jared. I need to know I have a job to go back to, a job that hasn't been…compromised by…" This was so awkward. She hated it.

"The investigation," Jared finished.

"Have you heard anything more?"

"Sam called this morning. You've been reinstated and cleared," he said. "I already sent letters to the people who matter most."

Haley's gaze flew to Jared's. "You wrote letters before you knew the outcome? Why?"

"It was the right thing to do. You're exonerated, Haley. Free."

Exonerated. Free. Not likely. There would always be some who looked at her and wondered, just like Jared. She looked up to find him watching her. "Were you going to tell me?"

"Yes. But I'll confess, I thought if you had nothing to go back to, you would stay."

"That wouldn't have been fair," she murmured.

"Nothing about meeting you has been fair." They rode to the sound of hooves against gravel and birds chirping in the pines. "I wish I'd met you first," he said.

She closed her eyes swaying with the horse's rhythm. *So do I, Jared. So do I. But you didn't and we're here and this is the way things are.*

"Thank you for the endorsements," she said. "I'll set up times for Sarah to come and visit Walt during school breaks."

"Will you come, too?"

"Probably not." She paused a moment, then continued. "There's something else I need you to answer."

"Ask," he said.

"Do you believe I hate that Mitch was killed?"

"Yes," he said without hesitation.

She stared into his eyes and saw truth. It didn't change the fact they had no future, but it lifted a huge weight from her heart. "Thank you. You have no idea how much this means to me."

He looked away. "I think I do." He moved his horse closer. Their legs bumped. "I'm not sorry for last night, only sorry that it made you uncomfortable. If I could, I'd do things differently from start to finish."

Start to finish. She didn't want to think about start or finish. She nudged her horse ahead, breaking contact, but Jared persisted, easing his animal into a matching pace.

"I'd like your opinion on a project I'm working on when we get back to the house," he said.

Longing pulled like a wire stretcher across her heart. She wanted to be part of his life, but she could never be what he deserved. Even if he loved her, Mitch would always stand in the middle. She couldn't stay and let her heart be stomped all over again. The cost was too high for everyone. They rode into the barnyard and put the horses away. She paused beside a box stall housing the most beautiful paint mare she'd ever seen.

"That's Calliope," Jared said. "Pretty, isn't she?"

Haley stroked the velvety nose, then ran her hands along the muscular neck. "She's beautiful. She wasn't here before or I'd have seen her." Haley looked at the mare's heavy sides. "She's in foal."

"Walt must have brought her in off pasture before they picked Sarah up," Jared said. "She's carrying the last of a long line of cutting horses. You might say next to Sarah, Calliope is the apple of Walt's eye."

Haley gave the mare's neck a final rub and turned away. "What did you want to show me?" she asked.

He held his hand out. She hesitated a moment, then took it. He led her toward the small office where she'd seen him sequestered for hours on end.

"What do you do in here?" she asked. Blueprints were scattered across a wide corner table.

"This is the bones of the ranching operation," he said. "Breeding and sales records, feed bills, supply lists. You know the drill. Come here. This is what I wanted to show you."

Haley looked at the blueprints. "Are you expanding the ranch?" It would be a shame to blight the land with more buildings, but this was none of her business. It wasn't her home.

"They're plans to expand the riding program," Jared said. "This is the new barn and arena. Animal programs can reach a lot of kids that people can't. This has been a dream of mine for a long time. It's a much needed ministry, Haley. These kids need to experience God's love as much as the rest of us, perhaps more because of their disabilities. If I can be a tool to show them the way…give them some hope and healing."

His voice choked.

Hope for the soul. Healing for the mind. Was there such a thing? Haley wasn't sure anymore. Jared turned a few blueprint pages and found the one he wanted. "What do you think?"

Haley stepped back and fingered the table edge. "I think it's a beautiful and noble cause, one that you'd be very good at, but you can't fix all things for all people, Jared."

"I can't, but with God's help, I can do something." He lifted his dark eyes to hers and studied her face, as though weighing whether he should say more. "I couldn't fix Mitch either, but God did."

The brightness of the day disappeared beneath a cloud of anger. "Why does nearly every conversation come back to Mitch? Maybe if you'd stop trying to fix everyone and just try to understand them, we'd all be better off." She backed toward the door, powerless to stop the flow. "Did you bring me here to share this dream of yours or to defend Mitch and make me see him differently so you could fix me, too?"

Jared laid the plans aside. "I didn't have an agenda. The plans were important to me and I wanted to share them with you."

She wanted to believe him.

"Your plan won't work. I'm not broken, Jared. That's something Mitch tried and failed at." Suspicion guarded her words.

"I want you whole and happy. That's all," he said.

He took a step toward her, but she retreated. One

hand rested on the door knob, ready to yank it open if he got too close.

"I wasn't unhappy before coming here. I'm not the one whose soul was sick. Mitch was," she snapped.

"I'm not going to defend Mitch. I can't." He crossed the office floor and put his hands on her shoulders. Her skin was warm beneath his fingers, but her eyes were flat and cold.

"It doesn't end there or you would never have looked for me. You always fix and finish things. You said so yourself. So did Walt." Jared's features hardened. Doom settled like a cloud inside the building.

Jared didn't really care about her welfare. She was only another object to add to his list of accomplishments. Another one of Mitch's broken toys that needed a crutch until they could walk again. The pain of it was unbearable. How many others were there?

"You have to have a cause to work on, don't you, Jared? Well, I am not a cause," she said, leashing her anger with short, controlled words. "Neither is my daughter."

His dark eyes softened, inviting her in. "No, you're not a cause," he said. "But I don't expect you to believe that. We could be partners, helping others. I see you disappearing, Haley. That would be a waste when I also see glimpses of the woman you are inside. The one who wants to come out but is afraid."

His words ripped into her soul like talons. "I…" The word trailed off, taking the thought with it. She wanted her life whole, not left in the fragments of

Mitch's waste. Wholeness lay within reach. All she had to do was grasp it. But not here. Not with Jared who looked at her as an unfinished project. She wanted his love, his heart, and wanting that was selfish in itself when she couldn't come to him pure and undefiled.

Dreams. A million little scenes flashed by in a split second, filled with joy, hope, sharing, but the final memory was so poignant she opened the door to escape. Mitch. He was the reason Jared saw her the way he did. Mitch had ruined any chance for her to be happy with any man. She would never be free and she couldn't be repaired.

"Don't waste your time on me, Jared. You can't help me. Mitch saw to that."

She saw her despair reflected in his eyes. "Dreams can be reshaped," he said. "Not every man is Mitch. I'm not, Haley. I would never hurt you."

She snapped inside. "Stop saying that. That's what Mitch said just before he raped me." She recoiled at voicing the word she'd danced around for eight years. Speaking it brought a release, however minor, but didn't lessen the vileness. "He used me and threw me away. The only good thing he ever did was leave me with Sarah. He killed a part of me that will never live again," she said with quiet fury. "Only Sarah matters."

Shock siphoned the blood from Jared's face. He gripped the desk chair, the horror of what she'd revealed written all over his face. He didn't see her anymore. He saw through her. The ugliness of

Mitch's act would forever stand between them, now. Nothing would be the same again.

A scuffle outside the window made her jump, then the door yanked open. Haley's stomach lurched to her throat. Walt stood behind the screen door, his face as white as the hair on his head. He wasn't supposed to be here.

"Jared," he whispered. His stricken eyes turned on Haley. "Mitch," he said softly. "Sarah." Anger flashed across his face. "You're lying." His voice cracked, then his feeble legs buckled. Haley reached for him, but he pulled away and stumbled. It was Jared who broke his fall.

Chapter Eleven

"What have I done?" Haley whispered. Her face turned chalky, her eyes deep pools of misery. "I never wanted this. Never wanted anyone to know."

Jared lifted Walt in his arms, but even his slight weight felt like a sack of boulders. Walt mumbled something and opened his eyes. Shock dulled his reflexes. "Not true," he muttered. Jared managed to pull the screen door open and carry Walt into the house.

"I'm sorry," Haley said, closing the door. Tears streamed down her face. "I'm so sorry. I never meant…"

"It's done, Haley," Jared said. One look at Walt's face made him wish it could be undone. But Walt's devastation didn't hold a candle to the pain he saw in Haley's eyes. "You didn't do anything wrong. Let's deal with one thing at a time." He laid Walt on the couch.

"She lied," Walt moaned, his head thrashing from

side to side. "Why would she do that?" His angry gaze impaled Haley. "We wanted you to stay here. Why would you do this?" He closed his eyes and whispered, "Sarah. You came because of Sarah."

"Walt, stop it," Jared said. Haley looked like she was about to collapse. Her shaking hands cupped her cheeks, but retaliation sparked her eyes. This was not the time for a showdown. "I'm sorry, Haley. He doesn't realize what he's saying."

"I do know," Walt said, falling back against the couch cushion.

If it had been anyone but Walt making the accusation, Jared had no doubt Haley would have used any means possible to defend herself. But it was Walt, and no doubt his frail health held her in check. She cast a fleeting look at Jared, then ran up the stairs. He should have defended her without hesitation. Now it was too late.

Mitch raped me.

She never wanted anyone to know.

Jared didn't want to wrap his mind around those words, but they kept repeating over and over like an old horror flick. In his heart he'd known, just hadn't wanted to conceive of something so ugly being done by someone he loved so much. He eased Walt back onto the couch and put a pillow behind his head.

"Stay here," Jared said. "And don't move."

"You're going after her?" Walt cried. "You know she's lying. Mitch wouldn't do such a thing."

"We don't know what Mitch was capable of before he came back, Walt," Jared said. "He was pretty messed up."

"But you can't believe…" Walt turned his face away.

Jared remembered the fear in Haley's eyes, the choked-off hurt and anger. He understood all of it now. Any doubt lingering in his mind dissolved. "I do believe, Walt. Have you taken a good hard look at her? There's no way she's lying about this. We should have helped her. All of us." He wished he'd conveyed that to her from the start. "I'll be back. Haley needs me."

He rushed up the stairs and twisted Haley's doorknob. It held. Heartrending sobs echoed under the door crack. "Haley, let me in." The crying quieted. He suspected she'd buried her face into a pillow to muffle the sound. "None of this matters to me."

Liar. It does matter. But we can deal with it.

"We'll work through this," he pleaded. "Open the door. We have to talk."

His stomach lurched at the thought of what more talk would reveal, but this wasn't about him. It was about the brother he'd never lost faith in—until now. It was about the vile act that had destroyed hope in the woman he'd come to cherish. It was about a future that had held a sliver of hope, and now seemed bleak and unattainable, tainted with memories that shouldn't matter, but did.

"It's too late, Jared. Go away. There's nothing left."

She sounded so close yet unreachable. Two inches

of door separated them. Those two inches seemed like a canyon span. He had to see her, hold her, take away the bad memories and give her new ones. *Please Lord God. Help me.*

He moved down the hall to Sarah's door and slipped inside to the bathroom that joined Sarah's room to Haley's. Haley hunched against her bedroom door with her legs drawn tight against her chest. Her cloud of silky hair hid what he knew was a face as ravaged as her soul.

He was losing her. If he didn't draw her back, he'd lose her forever. She'd disappear into her circle of pain and be lost.

"Haley?"

She jumped to her feet, her agony so tangible it stole his breath. "Get out," she choked. "I don't want you here."

"I'm not leaving you like this." He stepped into her room. The late-afternoon sun was hot on his back, casting a long shadow as he passed in front of the window. She watched the shadow approach with panic-widened eyes, then flattened herself against the door, groping for the lock, watching his shadow creep before him.

Jared backed off. He was bigger than her, stronger, and the last thing he wanted was to appear threatening. He stopped, hunkered down on his ankles and looked up. "I'm not going away until we talk this through," he said, softly, evenly.

"I said no. I don't want you here," she repeated.

"I don't want to talk. I just want to go home." Hysteria bubbled close to the surface.

He suspected her mind had flashed back. He felt her helplessness, her rage. He had to make her see him for who he was, not who she saw in her mind. "Haley. It's me, Jared. I'm not going anywhere."

For a split second, the shadows lifted from her eyes, then tears rolled down her cheeks. "I have nothing to give you."

"Then I won't ask for anything." He rose and hesitated a moment. Nothing in his entire life was more important than making her see him. If he bungled this, he'd lose her forever.

She wrapped her arms around herself. "I don't want to feel this way. I want to be normal."

Her eyes held a plea he couldn't ignore. He crossed the room in three strides and gathered her close. "Haley, Haley. We'll get through this. Let me help you."

For a moment, she yielded. He savored the feel of her in his arms. He would protect her forever, love her, help her heal. Her heart pounded in unison with his. Then she pushed back and beat clenched fists against his chest. Shadows haunted her eyes again. Her sobs grew louder.

She ducked around him, bolting like a green filly. "You can't help me. Don't you see? It's no good, Jared. I'm so sorry that Walt overheard. I'm so sorry about everything. I hadn't thought about Mitch in years until he showed up." She cast her gaze to the floor. "Since then, I've thought of little else."

She was pulling away and there wasn't a thing he could do to stop her. "Haley." This time he heard the plea in his own voice.

"Let's not do this," she said. "I'll see that Walt has time with Sarah, but I won't come back here, Jared. Don't ask me to, don't call. Just let it be. Let me go. Please."

He'd lost her. That stubborn pride that he so admired had aligned with her fear and defeated him. That she asked him to let her go meant he still had a minor foothold if he chose to press the matter. The thought tasted like gall. He looked deep into her eyes and saw years of hidden anguish culminated in this one moment. She'd suffered enough. He wouldn't add to it.

"This is what you really want?"

A tear rolled down her face, followed by another. "It's what I have to have. It's what I need."

What you need is someone to love you through this. Let me love you, Haley.

Longing, sadness and loss scattered from her like broken crystals. He knew in his heart that her decision was final. He could argue until the chickens roosted. Perhaps it was God's plan for him to be the instrument of forcing her to face her pain to move ahead without anything more. He swallowed hard, then nodded, accepting defeat. He crossed the room, opened the locked door and walked toward the stairs. A hollow echo followed his steps. Haley's door closed quietly behind him.

* * *

The sun rose like it did every morning, bathing the late-summer day with hues of orange and red. Jared found no joy in it. He smoothed the tattered letter on his desk, its edges a testimony to how often he'd poured over the words. His office door opened and he lifted his head.

"I can't believe they're gone," Adele said, closing the door behind her. "You look awful, Jared. Have you been in here all night?"

Jared nodded. "I couldn't sleep." The final scene in Haley's room had kept him pacing the floor for hours, his heart as empty as the room where she'd slept. "I came out here to work, but couldn't even do that."

"What is this?" Adele said, coming around the desk.

"A letter Mitch wrote. Carl Martin sent over a box of stuff Mitch left at the Fellowship Booth in Cheyenne. This was in it. It's postmarked six months ago." Jared set his elbows on his desk, then dropped his head into his hands.

"The letter doesn't mention Haley by name. Only what happened the night he met her." His voice hitched. He swallowed hard and continued. "I remember him saying that he'd done some awful things. Things he couldn't make right." Jared banged his fist on the desk. "Everything Haley said is true. I suspected. I knew, but I'd hoped. It's all here. Mitch's regret and sorrow, his need for forgiveness and fear of owning what he'd done." Tears stung Jared's eyes. He refused to let them fall. "I don't know what to do with this."

Adele moved to the other side of the desk without reading the letter. Her quiet strength filled the room, settling some of Jared's pent-up rage.

"You have to keep it, Jared. Put it away for now. At some point, Haley may need to see it to move past where she is. I don't know when that time will be, but you'll know."

Jared picked up a pencil and snapped it in his hand, the sick feeling inside him returning, along with anger he didn't know he was capable of.

Don't go to that place. Not yet.

He shoved Mitch from his mind. Mitch wasn't important. Haley was, and she'd made it clear she didn't want to see him again—ever.

"You saw Haley and Sarah before they left. Were they okay?" he asked.

"Sarah's angry and doesn't understand what all the tension is about, but she loves her mom. She will work through this and be okay. I'm not so sure about Walt. Or you and Haley." Adele's warm hand penetrated the coldness in his body. "God's healing happens in His own way and in His own time. Don't lose faith."

"She won't be back," Jared said. The knowledge twisted and turned inside him.

"You don't know that. She needs time. What happened with Mitch isn't eight years ago for Haley. In her mind, it's yesterday."

Jared's throat closed. Yes. And now he was supposed to do the same thing he'd once told Haley to do. Give this mess to God. That day seemed like a lifetime ago. He thought he'd done that. He hadn't appreciated the magnitude of his request until now. How did a person give violation to God and forge ahead? He tried to shut out the picture.

"I saw Walt drive off early this morning," he said. "Where did he go?"

"To see Pastor McDonald."

Jared nodded. "That's good."

"Maybe you should go, too," Adele said.

"Not now."

She reached across the desk and patted his hand. "I'm sorry. It's awful to watch someone you love suffer and not be able to do a thing to make it better. You do love her, don't you?"

Jared nodded, then leaned against his desk and cradled his head in his hands again. The place Haley had filled in his heart was ravaged and empty. Her voice echoed in the dark chamber.

Go away. I can't give you what you need. I never should have come here. I don't want to see you again.

He processed every reaction and word, every look and piece of body language, from the time he'd run into her in Cheyenne outside the Fellowship Booth to last night. Finally he understood the depth of her despair, the source of her hopelessness.

It was the legacy she'd left him. He pressed his fingers deeper into his temple, trying to squeeze from his mind the horror of her confession, erase the picture of what Mitch had done to her and the terror she must have felt, the sounds of her anguished cries as she'd sobbed her misery into the darkness. The thoughts circled in his mind, chasing the flat words of Haley's confession.

His mother's hand breached the coldness in his body. "Does she know how you feel?"

Jared shook his head. "She knows I wanted her to stay."

"And how did she respond?"

"She left and didn't look back. I think that pretty much says it all."

"This isn't about you, Jared," Adele chided gently. "You matter. That's part of why she's so hurt. She isn't in a place to really hear you right now." She tapped his hand. "She will. You did the most important thing. You left Walt and went after her. That's what she'll remember. Not right away, but when the pain settles. Give her time to recognize that you see *her*, not what Mitch *did* to her." She gave his hand a final squeeze and walked to the door.

Jared lifted his head. Letting go would require every bit of grit and prayer in him, but it was what she wanted. He'd do it, with God's help. "I love her enough to let her go, but I'll never give up on her," he said, the weight of the decision heavy on his heart.

"I'd be very disappointed in you if you did. Let me know if there's some way I can help," she said, her smile reaching her eyes.

"You already have."

"Haley may be out of our reach, but she's never

out of God's. He doesn't give up on any of us." She rose and slipped through the door.

Jared watched her walk to the house then picked up the phone and dialed Sam McIntosh's number. He'd already taken the necessary steps to reinstate her reputation and secure her livelihood, but it wouldn't hurt to go above and beyond.

If Haley wouldn't let him be a direct part of her life, he'd stay in the background and watch from a distance. He could live with her loss, as long as she was okay—as long as her wounds healed and she was happy again.

September sneaked in like a baby's sigh, bringing cooler nights and shorter days. Haley usually looked forward to fall and a lighter travel schedule, but this time, she coveted work. Anything to keep Jared's memory at bay. Even Hap seemed at a loss to know what to do with her. He tiptoed around her as if uncertain what might set her off.

Every few days, flowers arrived from Jared with cards she refused to read. Never in her life had anyone given her flowers. She pretended not to care, telling Hap to throw them away and threatening to refuse further deliveries, but a warm glow flowed through her that Jared hadn't forgotten or tossed her away.

She would touch the petals, drink in the rich fragrance when no one was around, and when blooms wilted and the stems turned brown, Hap would toss them in the trash. Her heart would break all over again, which was stupid. They were just flowers and they were dead. Sarah caught her once lifting an unopened card from the trash.

"You're upset all the time because you love Uncle Jared," Sarah had said. "He loves you, too. I know he does. He asks about you all the time. Why can't we be a family?"

Haley couldn't tell her why without destroying her small world. She'd fought back tears, and Sarah had stormed away. Haley had plucked a yellow rose that hadn't yet died, carried it to her room and pressed it between the pages of *A Tale of Two Cities*.

Collecting a fading bloom from each bouquet had become a ritual now, along with the message cards she still couldn't bring herself to read.

Once, when Jared had called Sarah, Haley picked up the extension just to hear his voice. Sometimes she thought she'd caught glimpses of him at a few rodeos, but it had to be an illusion, a figment of her imagination, and when she searched for him, she never found him.

The truth was, she loved him. If she had any doubts before, they'd vanished after her rushed flight home and the magnitude of telling him to leave her alone settled in. The ugliness of rape would always stand between them. How could Jared move past it if she couldn't? He deserved better.

You can move past it, but you can't do it alone.

The thought stayed with her while she parked her old camper near the Rangely rodeo grounds, waved a greeting to a few familiar faces and set about securing her campsite. Local rodeos didn't pay as much as the bigger ones, but the work was steady and the participants like family. Work was what she needed now. She was more than grateful Sam had called.

She'd traveled alone before, but this was the first time that it gnawed at her like a mouse on a rope. The days were busy and exhausting, but the nights… The nights were endless.

Sarah had refused to come. The distance between them hurt almost as much losing Jared. She remembered every whisper, every touch, from the day they'd first met until now.

"Stop it," she whispered. "It was over before it even started." The ache in her soul seemed endless.

Sunday provided a lull in activity. The last events were scheduled after lunch and ran into early evening. She wandered restlessly around the campsites, then strolled over to the area where Cowboy Church was set up. She hadn't been to a service since going with Jared and she didn't really want to go now, but the thought of being alone with herself in her present state of mind wasn't appealing either. If the service made her uncomfortable, she'd leave.

The sun dipped below the horizon. Campfires filled the air with the smells of coffee and bacon. Laughter and the sound of strumming guitars surrounded the camp. People milled around, some joining other campfires, others heading toward the area set aside for the service. A few called and waved to her, but still, she'd never felt lonelier in her life.

She jammed her hands into her jean pockets and followed the crowd. Soft music played inside the makeshift tent. She recognized the old hymn, "Amazing Grace," Pop's favorite. Memories rushed back of rodeos past, before Jared or Sarah or Mitch. Her faith had been simple then, happy and filled with contentment.

She'd confessed herself a sinner in need of the saving grace of The One who died and rose again to redeem her, believed that the goodness of God dwelt in those who believed. She'd trusted with her whole heart and soul in a jealous God who protected His own. Right up until Mitch, the trial by fire where she'd disappeared in the ashes along with her faith.

The strains of music surrounded her, the old hymn pounded into her mind.

Why couldn't she think of Jared without remembering that Mitch had stolen the one thing she had to offer the man she loved, herself, her purity? *Lord, God, I needed You. Why weren't You there?*

"You going in?" someone murmured from behind.

"I'm not sure," Haley said, stepping aside to let him pass. A few moments later, she edged into a back row and sat down on a folding chair. Pop had been disappointed when she'd quit attending church and the rodeo tent meetings. He and Sarah had gone without her. She felt like she'd lost a part of him. Now she felt his presence along with something more, Someone more. Someone higher.

The music stopped and a young man stepped to the front. He smiled at the small crowd and welcomed them. Haley fidgeted, dipping her chin to let her hair hide her face. The song service began but she didn't join. She studied the profiles of those caught up in the worship of music, their joyous faces lifted in praise. They looked content, peaceful.

The young man ended the song. A hush fell inside the tent. He began slowly, "Elizabeth Elliott once said that in the hard lessons of life, God wants to give us Himself."

The words drew Haley in spite of her resolve to not take anything he said to heart. His next words hit her like a gut punch.

"I had intended to speak on the greatness of God's love this morning, but He gave me another message instead. I'd like to share with you about the groaning of God. There is an appointed time for everything, and God notes our sufferings. His Spirit prays for us with groaning which cannot be uttered."

Haley tried to stem a rush of hurt. If God noted her suffering, why hadn't He done anything about it?

The young minister glanced around the small gathering, his warmth and energy filling the space. "Many of us have been in tough spots—heartrending situations that have tested our faith. I want you to know that it's okay to struggle. What we have to recognize is that searching for an escape doesn't leave us any strength to endure what God is asking us to go through."

Haley edged to the end of her seat as he talked about suffering being only for this present time and how people's sufferings are not wasted.

"Glory will come," he'd said. "But until the glory, we groan."

He talked about staying focused on the glory as people groan over the suffering in this world and how the Spirit of God focuses on the glory, yet groans, praying for them because they don't always know how—feeling with them—and groaning with uttering too deep for words.

A gentle urgency stirred in Haley's heart. The man encouraged everyone who suffered to not abandon their walk with the Lord to join the enemy of their souls, but to focus on the glory awaiting them.

His eyes seemed to look straight into Haley's soul as he quietly ended his message with, "It's okay to groan and grieve 'in hope.' Allow the Spirit of God to comfort you. Trust His prayers on your behalf, prayers that are too deep for words."

Haley barely moved as the final song stirred the faith she'd buried with her innocence. The song talked about all things working for good and trusting God's heart when one can't see His hand. Just what was in God's heart for her?

The music ended. People shuffled out of the tent. For the first time in a long while, she wanted to be alone. She wanted time to think. Time to test the shaky ground the message had encouraged her to explore. Haley pushed back into the chair. If she were invisible, the world would go away and leave her alone. But that wasn't what she wanted or needed. She needed to think about what she'd heard. Really think. She tucked her chin, listening to the sounds of people shuffling outside the tent.

"Is there something I can help you with? Anything I can do?"

The young minister's voice forced her to lift her head. Compassion radiated from his eyes.

Haley's eyes welled. "Pray for me," she murmured.

"I will," he said quietly.

Unnerved by his words as well as her request, she rose and hurried into the cool night air. A man studied the bulls near the pens, his chin resting on the rail. She'd lost count of the nights she'd stood in the same spot, studying the bulls before competition, vowing to keep the riders safe no matter what.

The man shifted, the sun outlining his profile, then he pushed his hat back with a familiar gesture that stirred her memory. She watched a moment longer, then walked slowly back toward the camper, wondering if images of Jared would always haunt her in how others carried themselves. She hadn't realized what a powerful opponent love could be.

Chapter Twelve

Sleep was as elusive as happily ever after, but one picture stayed in the foreground of Haley's mind through that night and the next. It wasn't Jared, Mitch, or the events of that disastrous night eight years ago, but an image of the Spirit of God praying on her behalf because she couldn't believe enough to pray for herself anymore.

A sliver of the old faith she'd held as a child stole into the darkness, drawing her toward the light. She pulled Pop's Bible out of the drawer and laid it beside her unable to remember the last time she'd turned the pages. Maybe it was time. Maybe the questions she needed answered lay within these pages. As soon as she finished her work, she'd search for some answers.

She flung the sleeping bag aside and padded to the door, shivering as her bare feet hit the floor. She readied herself for the day's events, then flipped the lock and pushed the door open. A mist hung over the rodeo grounds, the sun beginning to tease the skyline. The bull pens and campground buzzed with activity. A morning chill nipped her skin. She rubbed her arms, grabbed some jerky and trail mix from the truck, then saw two familiar figures crossing the parking lot. Her chest tightened.

Walt and Adele. How had they known where to find her?

Hap.

Please, God, don't let there be another scene like before. None of us could bear it.

Her pulse ceased to pound. Anxiousness evaporated in the morning mist, leaving only a sense of wonder. Her plea was sincere. Had God actually heard and calmed her anxiety? Would He hear again?

Help me protect Sarah without hurting Walt and Adele any more than I already have.

Haley drew strength from the quietness of spirit that remained. She half expected this newfound calmness to disappear, but it didn't. She lifted her chin and waited for Walt and Adele to reach her campsite.

Adele rushed forward, gathering Haley in a welcoming embrace. Her first instinct was to back off and keep her defenses up, but the emotion Adele generated was warm and loving.

"I've missed you," Adele said. "I'd be lying if I said I haven't been worried. How are you?"

"I'm good," Haley fibbed.

She stepped away, avoiding Adele's gaze that saw far more than Haley wanted. She looked directly at

Walt, refusing to cower behind the pain of their last encounter.

Before her stood the broken man she'd seen when she first arrived at Jared's ranch—before Sarah's presence penetrated his grief and gave him hope. She remembered the day she'd seen them bent over a chessboard, Sarah's dark hair contrasting with Walt's snowy crop. Sarah hated chess, but she'd played to please Walt, and the two were in stitches over some silly move Sarah had made. Walt's eyes had sparkled with joy.

Now he looked years older. She'd brought a permanent sadness into his life with her ill-timed confession. He hadn't deserved that.

"I'm sorry I hurt you," she said. "There's nothing more I can say to make the truth easier."

"I wish you could tell me it never happened, but I know better," Walt said. "Jared made me see. He's always looked out for Mitch, but this time…"

Haley flinched. Walt didn't voice the rest of his thoughts, but Haley knew what he was thinking. Jared fixed Mitch's messes. This was one he couldn't do anything about.

"Is Jared with you?" she asked.

"No," Adele said. "He's at a cattle buyer's meeting."

Haley's heart deflated. She was one of Mitch's messes and since she wouldn't see him, he'd sent Walt and Adele in his place.

Oh, Jared.

She closed her eyes and felt his touch, heard his laugh. It hurt to think of him. In retrospect, she knew he'd stood up to his family on her behalf because she'd had no one else. He felt responsible for her.

He wanted to right what Mitch had wronged even if it meant bringing her to his ranch and making her a part of his life—a partner. She wanted more than that. What she wanted and what she could deliver were worlds apart. Jared would martyr himself for her and Sarah. That's the type of man he was. She loved him for it, but would never accept it. She opened her eyes. Walt watched her, his gray gaze filled with sadness. She had to say something.

"You didn't need to come all this way to tell me you believe me." Silence hung like the morning mist. "Sarah is your granddaughter, Walt. You don't have to be afraid that I'll keep her from you. I would never use her against you. I know you would never use her against me."

Walt stepped forward. "I know. What I came for doesn't concern Sarah. It's about you and me." He gripped his fingers, pulling nervously at them. "I need to say this in person and it couldn't wait any longer." He looked straight into Haley's eyes. "I accused you, doubted you, blamed you because I didn't want to see my son the way you saw him." He let his hands fall to his sides. "There is no excuse for the things I said." He paused a moment, catching his breath. "I talked with my pastor. Adele and I spent hours praying for God's peace. I believe you, Haley. And I want you to know how very sorry I am for what my son…" His voice choked. "Can you forgive me?"

Tears flowed down Walt's face. Shock wedged words in Haley's throat. She touched her own cheeks, surprised to find them wet. Walt opened his arms. She hesitated a moment, then followed her instincts and embraced him. The warmth of forgiveness flooded her like whitewash on an old fence, rejuvenating, renewing.

"Thank you for this," she whispered. "I do forgive you."

Her heart released a pocket of pain. Walt needed her forgiveness as much as she needed his. She admitted the truth with grace and hope. When she let him go, part of the hurt she'd carried like a shield left, too. For a moment, she felt as if she'd sprouted wings and could fly. Tears filled her eyes again.

So this is what it feels like to forgive.

"Will you stay and have breakfast with me?" she said, her voice choking. "I'll try not to burn it."

Breakfast was serene. Haley wanted it to last. The only people missing were Hap, Sarah and Jared. She must mend the rift with Sarah. And Jared, too, but she couldn't, wouldn't think about him right now.

Walt approached her while Adele started to clean up. "There's one more thing I'd like to ask you," he said, his head humbly bent. "It concerns Sarah."

She nodded. "Okay."

"The mare, Calliope. I'd like Sarah to have her. And the foal, too. She was Mitch's horse. I realize you might not want any reminders of him around, but Calliope's wonderful, and the foal is the last of its line." Walt hesitated. "If you'd rather not, I understand."

Haley looked into his eyes. He did understand, and oddly, the discomfort she expected to feel wasn't there. Maybe there was hope for her after all. "I think Sarah would love that. Thank you, Walt."

"Thank you, for Sarah. She's a rose, Haley. Seems we always thank God for the roses, but we never thank Him for the thorns that come with them. I never saw the value in the thorns before." Adele joined him and they turned to go. "I'll make the arrangements for Calliope as soon as she foals."

Haley leaned against the camper long after they'd driven out of sight. So much had happened in so short a time. She couldn't think about Jared without feeling his loss. She headed for the rodeo grounds with Walt's words ringing in her mind.

I never saw the value in the thorns.

Haley threw herself into facing bulls and racing barrels but nothing eased her restless spirit. At night, something tugged inside her, a gentle plea, beckoning, offering something more than a lonely fire on a chilly evening. Mitch was her thorn, and she didn't want to see any value in him. But the truth was, without Mitch there would be no Sarah.

The thorn and the rose.

What would it cost her to forgive Mitch? Her body shuddered. She stoked the fire. Jared's face danced in the flames, then twisted in the smoke and disappeared. She loved him beyond a shadow, but he wasn't in love with her. He was cleaning up after Mitch. But for Mitch, what might have been? But for Mitch, she would never have met Jared. But for Mitch, she would never have had Sarah.

Oh, God. Why couldn't I have met Jared first? Why couldn't Sarah be his?

Only the snap of the logs and the singing crickets answered. She separated the coals and entered the camper. Her father's picture smiled down at her. The photo wavered in a watery gaze.

Her heart shattered. She climbed onto the bedspread and curled up in a ball, sobbing her misery into the pillow. Pop's worn Bible lay unopened on the bed where she'd left it a few days ago. Outside, a rumble of thunder threatened. She felt the coming storm deep inside her and her heart skipped.

It was as though two people struggled inside her, each wanting her to go in a different direction. If she wanted peace, she must confront the issues warring for her soul. She must confront herself, her anger at Mitch and most of all her feelings for Jared.

Outside the window, gray clouds swirled. Thunder shook the camper. She pressed her fingers against her temples. Sarah was born on a day much like this; a day filled with anguish and joy; a day that sometimes led to darker thoughts. How she craved peace in her soul, for an answer to the why of Mitch and the ache of Jared. She opened Pop's Bible and flipped a page, memories dropping like rain. Did God feel her turmoil? Was he praying for her, like the young minister had said? She fanned the pages and found a card stuck in the center.

She pulled it out and laid the open Bible on the bed, noting the tattered edges of the page. Pop must have sought comfort here often. Maybe she would find some, too. An underlined passage stood out.

"I am fearfully and wonderfully made." She whispered the words.

Sarah's face formed in Haley's mind. She closed her eyes, then sought the page again and continued reading.

"My frame was not hidden from You when I was made in secret and skillfully wrought in the depths of the earth."

The sense of terror she'd felt so long ago flashed through her. God had seen. All these years she'd thought God had shut out her pleas because she'd disobeyed Pop in going to the carnival and flirting with Mitch.

She'd felt she'd brought misfortune on herself as well as Pop. She knew what happened wasn't all her fault, but part of it was. She'd called for God then. He hadn't answered. Why hadn't He rescued her from the thorn? Her eyes darted back to the page, needing to understand, needing to let go of the burden always weighting her down even when she thought it didn't.

"Your eyes have seen my unformed substance and in Your book they were all written, the days that were ordained for me, when as yet there was not one of them. How precious are Your thoughts to me, O God. How vast is the sum of them. If I should count them they would outnumber the sand."

Her voice faded in a clap of thunder. She sat up like a lightening bolt and hugged her knees. The truth of the written Word lit the darkness in her heart.

In Your book they were written, the days that were ordained for me.

For Sarah. For Mitch.

She picked up the card she'd pulled from the center of Pop's Bible and turned it over. A sticky note with Pop's handwriting brought tears to her eyes. She held it close.

"My beautiful Haley. I trust you will find this in God's time, and that it will bring you the healing of soul I have long prayed for and fulfill the purpose God ordained for both you and Sarah. I love you both so much. Pop."

The words wavered through her tears. She opened up the envelope. Pop had underlined a quote, noting the words came from *The Purpose Driven Life*. Haley whispered the words, letting them settle in her soul.

"You were conceived in the mind of God. He thought of you first. It is not fate nor chance nor luck nor coincidence that you are breathing at this very moment. You are alive because God wanted to create you."

Haley's eyes widened. Sarah was here because God wanted her here. And He wanted her here in the very fashion He had ordained for both of them—for a bigger purpose that she had chosen to bury beneath anger and pain. Reality hurtled her back to earth. Two giant teardrops rolled down her cheeks. But what purpose? She hadn't bothered to try to find out.

"I'm sorry, so sorry. I missed it. Everyone else saw, but I missed it. Oh, Lord God, I'm ready to see the value of the thorn."

The peace she'd known as a child washed through her, then Mitch's plea echoed in her memory.

Forgive me. Forgive yourself.

She tucked Pop's note and card back into the passage and closed it. She wasn't ready to wrap her mind around forgiving Mitch, not yet. But the anger and pain were gone, leaving her free to explore the possibility. All that needed closure was Jared. No matter where she was or what she did, he was never far from her thoughts.

"I love you, Jared," she whispered. The patter of rain beat against the camper. Haley's tears fell, too.

Be my partner, he'd said.

If she was to find God's purpose in the trials He'd placed in her path, she must let go of Jared and free him of his need to rescue her. She had to see him again, talk to him one more time. Release him. For Sarah's sake and her own.

Three days later, Haley arrived at Jared's house long after dark. A sense of coming home swamped her. She gripped the steering wheel, determined to see this through. She parked away from the house and stepped into the chilly night air. The porch light was on, but the house appeared dark and deserted.

She hadn't told anyone but Hap about her plan to see Jared again. She'd sworn him to silence, leaving less time for questions from Sarah and rehearsed speeches on Jared's part. She needed to gauge his reactions without prep time. Now it appeared no one was home.

She walked toward the barn. Surely someone was holding vigil with Calliope. Jared wouldn't leave the mare alone for long, especially this close to giving birth. She opened the barn door and entered. A low moan rose from Calliope's stall. Fear squeezed Haley's heart.

She hurried down the aisle as fast as she dared. The mare lay on her side, the hair along her flanks and sides heaving with each labored breath. Thin flecks of sweat formed around her eyes. How long she'd labored, Haley could only guess, but the window of time between safe and critical was slipping away. The mare couldn't last much longer. Where was everyone?

"Easy, girl," she crooned, rubbing her hands over the mare's side. "We'll have to do this together."

She'd never delivered a foal on her own before, but everything she'd watched Hap do came back in a flash. She moved around the mare's head along her back to her hindquarter and saw one tiny foot covered in a thin bluish-white sac. Haley swallowed hard. There should be two.

Panic gripped her. *Think, Haley. What would Hap do?*

Calliope struggled to rise, then fell back into the straw. If the foal's other leg remained hung-up, both would die. Haley reached for the emergency kit outside Calliope's stall and slipped her arm into a set of elbow length plastic gloves. Her experience stopped here. If she did something wrong, the mare would die. If she did nothing, they'd die anyway. And she'd be responsible.

"Help me, Lord. Send Jared. Send anyone."

Calliope groaned, her sleek body slippery with sweat. The window of safety closed. Haley waited for the contraction to end, then felt for the foals bent leg. She had to untangle it. She had to do it now.

A door banged outside.

"Jared. Shorty. Anyone. I'm in here. I need help," she called. The barn door slammed open.

"Haley?" Jared's quick steps rustled the barn shavings.

"Here." She shifted in the straw. "Calliope's in a bad way."

In an instant, he was there, standing behind her.

A cry of relief broke from her lips. Jared was here. Everything would be okay. "The leg is hung up," she said. "What do I do?"

"Follow the leg line with your hand. Feel where it's bent back."

Jared's calm voice didn't settle her fear. Haley pulled back. "I can't. Where were you? If she dies…"

"She won't die." His certainty bolstered her courage. "You have to finish this. There's no time. Feel for the knee."

"It's here. I feel it. It's bent."

"Follow it to the end of the foot. See if you can free it and straighten it out."

Haley gritted her teeth and felt for the tiny hoof. Heat penetrated the thin plastic glove. The mare's body contracted and tightened. Haley panicked.

"Wait it out," Jared said calmly. "Then push back and straighten the leg."

She waited. The pressure around her arm subsided. She pushed on the leg, moving it a fraction. Calliope moaned again, a deep wracking sound that brought tears to Haley's eyes. "Easy, girl," she crooned. "It's going to be okay." She pushed again. The leg gave. "I got it."

"Good girl." His voice held a faint tremor. "Now ease the leg out, grab them both and pull with the next contraction."

She grabbed the tiny hooves and waited, then pulled with everything inside her. The foal slid into the straw. Calliope moaned again. The foal was silent.

"No. Oh, no," Haley murmured.

Jared knelt in the straw. Using his sleeve, he wiped the sac from the foal's nose, then breathed air into the lifeless body. The small chest rose. Once, twice, three times.

Calliope staggered to her feel, pawing the ground. Haley pulled the glove off and stroked the mare's quivering body. Her gaze fixed on the foal's still, small form.

"Please, Lord. Let him live," she murmured.

She watched Jared work, and dared to hope that God would answer her prayer. One tiny hoof moved. Then both front feet twitched. A hesitant snort vibrated the small nostrils. Calliope nickered. The foal answered. Haley let the tears fall. "Thank You," she murmured, lifting her eyes toward heaven.

Jared waited a few more seconds, then swirled iodine around the navel area. Calliope nuzzled her baby, licking him, encouraging him to stand with short, low calls. Jared's arm slid around her waist.

"You did it. You saved them both," he said.

Haley rubbed her hands down her jeans. "Oh, Jared. I was so scared. Why wasn't someone here? Where were you?"

"The generator on the well pump went out. Calliope was fine when Shorty and I went to work on it. Then I decided to come back and check on her."

"Where's Walt and Adele?"

"Rapid City. They'll be back later tonight," he said, pulling her closer.

Haley realized she was trembling.

Jared guided her toward the stall door. "Let's give mother and son some time to bond before we move them to a clean stall."

Haley gripped his hands. "I don't want to leave. Can't we just sit in the corner and watch them for a while?"

He turned her around, lifting her face with his finger, then erased her tears with his thumbs. She leaned into his chest, letting his strength flow into her.

"I thought they were both going to die," she said. "It would have been my fault. Like Mitch."

Jared held her tighter. She melted into him, wanting to stay, knowing she couldn't.

"Mitch wasn't your fault," he said softly. "Mitch wasn't anyone's fault. It was just his time."

She knew he was right. "It's hard to let go of it." She felt his dark eyes watching her, probing for answers she wasn't sure she had.

"Why are you here, Haley? Why did you come back?"

A tremor ripped through her straight to his heart. He'd hoped she'd returned because she'd come to her senses and realized she couldn't live without him any more than he wanted to live without her. She ducked her chin and backed away, dashing that hope. Her gaze flew to his. The air between them crackled.

"I came to see you."

His heart nearly stopped. Had God finally answered his prayers? He took her hand, led her to a corner of Calliope's stall and sat down. She kept enough distance so their bodies didn't touch.

"Why? Why did you need to see me?" he asked.

She broke a piece of straw between her fingers. "Because I want you to know that I understand why you asked me to move here and be your partner."

"What is it you think you understand, Haley?"

Her eyes turned to deep amethyst in the shadowed stall. "I know that family is important to you. The most important thing in your life next to God." She hesitated, watching Calliope and the foal. "I know that you've spent a lifetime looking out for Mitch, fixing his mistakes, cleaning up his messes. Walt said so."

She looked straight at him. "You said so, too. I want you to know that you don't need to fix Mitch's mistakes. God has taken care of that for me. I just have to trust Him for the rest. I still have some things to work through, but I release you, Jared. You have no obligation to either me or Sarah."

Jared shifted to face her. His heart soared, then anger flashed through him, the storm before the calm. "Obligation. Is that what you think? That I wanted you here so I could fix what Mitch screwed up?"

"Isn't it?" Her luminous eyes shimmered with tears.

Jared scooted closer, taking her cold hands in his. "You don't know me very well at all, do you, Haley Clayton?"

She shook her head, dropping her gaze. "That's just the point. We don't know each other."

"I know that I love you for who you are, not because of what Mitch did or what you've endured because of it. I know that you're a warm, loving woman and mother with a heart as big as a Colorado mountain. I know I want to give you all the things I think you've longed for and you think you don't deserve. You are God's gift to me. I don't want to lose you, Haley. Ever." Her hand shook in his. "Look at me."

She raised her downcast eyes. He saw a shimmer of hope and her fear of reaching for it. He cupped her face in his hands.

"I love you. It doesn't matter to me what it took to make you into that person. I love you." He brushed his thumbs against her soft skin.

Her heart dropped. The tangy scent of his cologne filled the stall. She wanted nothing more than to believe, to have the right to claim his arms around her, to feel his protection along with the love shining from his eyes. He lifted his hand, gently pushing her hair from her shoulder.

"I prayed," she whispered. "It's taken me a long time, but I prayed for God to show me a purpose for the pain. I still can't see it, Jared."

"Sometimes we're so busy banging our head against a closed window we don't see the one that's opened across the room."

She closed her eyes. Jared said he loved her and she'd run away from him, but she'd come back. Was it really for the reason's she'd stated? *I love you. I see you,* he had said. Panic rose to her throat along with the shadow of memory. This was Jared. He wouldn't hurt her. She could give him anything but what he wanted most, herself.

"You deserve more than I can give you," she said.

"I deserve what God has put in front of me. So do you. It wasn't chance that brought you into my life. Yes, I sought you out for all the wrong reasons. But God brought you back to me for all the right ones."

He touched her face. "You said you don't see a purpose for the pain. I believe God's purpose was us, working together as one to show others the way to His saving grace."

The veil lifted from her eyes, letting her see what God had put before her from the beginning, His work, His way, with the man of His choosing.

"You've told me why you came," he said. "I have a question for you." He took her face in his hands again. "Do you love me, Haley?"

A draft teased her hair, blowing strands across her face. He captured them, caressing them between his fingers. She leaned into his touch.

"This isn't a trick question," he said, a smile pulling at his mouth. "Do you love me?"

"Yes," she murmured, looking down. "I love you. I have for a long time. I was just so afraid."

"Do you trust me?"

She gazed into his eyes and saw all the dreams of the future reflected back at her. Their future.

"Yes," she murmured. "I trust you." The admission released Mitch's final hold. *The truth will set you free.* So this was God's plan all along. She'd been too blind to see.

Jared crushed her to him. "I know you have fears. We'll work through them. Don't ever leave me again, Haley."

He claimed her lips. She surrendered not just her fears, but her heart and all that lay within.

"This isn't going to be easy," she said, wanting

him to be sure. "I have…lots of issues. You can still walk away."

Jared smiled. "Not a chance. Everyone has issues. Isn't it amazing what God allows us to go through so that one person might come to know His grace and love?"

She'd never looked at her life in quite that fashion until now. Jared was right. She had a lot to offer. She'd been to the edge and back. She could show others the way to find the light hidden by the darkness. She searched Jared's face. The love in his heart reflected in his eyes, erasing all doubt.

"I'm not going anywhere, Haley." He fished into his pocket and pulled out a small black box. "I've been carrying this thing around for weeks, afraid to put it in a drawer for fear that I wouldn't have it when you finally came to your senses. Will you marry me, Haley?"

"You never said you wanted to marry me before."

"I couldn't. I had to let God do His work in your life first. It was the only way." He pulled the ring from the box. "I think it's about time this found its rightful place in the world."

He took her hand. "Haley Clayton, will you honor me by being my wife, sharing my life and helping me build our dreams for the rest of our lives?"

She didn't hesitate a second. "Yes, Jared. I will."

He slid the amethyst on her finger. She belonged to him. He belonged to her. She had only God to thank for this precious gift, this miracle of love. She shifted, leaning against Jared's chest. Calliope's foal inched closer. Haley reached out, touching his velvety nose. The solitaire sparkled in the dim light.

"So what are you going to call this bundle of curiosity?" Jared asked.

"Miracle," she whispered. "Because God performed a miracle in my heart, and I'll never forget it. Every time I look at him, I'll remember." She stared at the ring, not wanting to break the moment. "Didn't you think you were taking an awful big chance that I might not come back, or say no?"

She felt him chuckle. "With God on our side, how could you say no?" He folded his arms around her and nuzzled her ear. "How do you think Sarah will feel about changing her name to Sinclair?"

"I think she'll be thrilled."

"Then let's phone Hap and our daughter and tell them the news."

Epilogue

Spring. The time of new life. New beginnings. The smell of wildflowers drifted in the air. Haley drew in their scent and let Spinner cross the field at his own pace, the letter Jared had given her crumpled in her hand. She'd come full circle.

The past two months being married to Jared had been the happiest of her life. Sarah was ecstatic. Hap was content in the guest house, sharing chores with Jared's foreman. Jared was adding a wing onto the house for Walt and Adele. Life was good, and she was grateful to God for His gifts. So why did the issue of Mitch have to come into play again now?

She lifted her eyes to the sky, half wishing God would speak in an audible voice and make it plain and clear, but she already knew the answer in her heart.

Because to completely forgive herself and be free of the past she had to forgive Mitch. Because forgiveness was a choice she had chosen to place on the back burner.

Months of praying, counseling and soul-searching had shown her the importance of forgiveness. So had Jared, in the way he never pushed but let her come to terms in her own time. She trusted him—trusted he would never do anything to harm her. That's why he'd given her Mitch's letter. Because he knew it didn't have the power to hurt her anymore.

She dismounted and settled in the grass, then pulled the letter from the battered envelope. The words leaped from the page, Mitch's anguish touching her in a way she'd never expected. She'd wanted him to suffer, told him so that day in the hospital. Now she knew how deeply he had, and it brought no satisfaction. She'd have been worried if it had.

A huge tear splattered on the page. She closed her eyes.

"I'm sorry, Mitch. Sorry for both of our pain. I do forgive you."

The final burden lifted from her heart. She was free and the issue of what to tell Sarah about her father was settled. As far as she was concerned, the matter was finished. She rose, put the letter back in the envelope and picked up Spinner's reins. She turned toward the house and saw Jared making his way toward her. She broke into a run, Spinner trotting alongside.

Jared met her halfway through the meadow. She threw her arms around him and held him close.

"It's over," she whispered. "I love you, Jared. I'll love you forever."

He looked into her eyes, all the love in his heart

shining there for her to see, then his head dipped and he claimed her lips. The shadow of a hawk sailed above them and Haley was certain God smiled.

* * * * *

Dear Reader,

Truly living for others requires daily dying to ourselves. At some point, forgiveness becomes an issue that confronts us all, whether it is a need to be forgiven or whether we are the ones who must do the forgiving. The wounds on our souls can be deeply emotional and devastating or relatively minor. In either case, we must choose whether to embrace a bitter spirit or experience the release forgiveness brings. Whichever path we choose will change us.

During our darkest times we tend to push God away. We feel He has abandoned us and we blame Him for our troubles, when in truth He is as close as He was to Jesus when Jesus hung on a cross to pay for our sins. Forgiving is never easy and doesn't happen overnight, but the release that comes with the action is well worth the effort.

My prayer is that anyone who embraces an unforgiving spirit will reap the benefits of or from forgiveness, no matter what the wrong, no matter who is right. May you seek God and find Him a willing advocate for a weary soul.

God bless each of you.

QUESTIONS FOR DISCUSSION

1. What was the truth that finally set Haley free?

2. Why do you think Haley chose the profession of rodeo clown, and what significance, if any, do you see from her clown makeup and costume?

3. What do you think prompted Haley to keep a child conceived from rape rather than give that child away?

4. At what point does Jared let go of his need for justice and allow God to use him to help Haley? What areas can you let go of in your own life for God to use you more effectively?

5. The Bible says perfect love casts out fear. How did Jared use his love for Haley to deal with her fears and how did it change him? How can God's unconditional love change us?

6. At what point did Walt realize the damage Mitch had done and how did this realization change how he viewed Haley? How do each of us handle the disappointments with friends and family and still honor God by our reactions?

7. Bad things happen in life to people who don't

seem to deserve them. Why is it so easy to lose our faith during those times and why do you think we blame God instead of the one who is the destroyer of our souls?

8. Why do you think God measures our trials by His strength, not our own?

9. What do you feel is the lesson behind the rose and the thorn?

10. At what point did Jared realize that praying for people was more important than "fixing" them? How can we change our prayer life to help others instead of "fixing" them, which is God's job?

11. What finally brings Haley to the realization that she is worthy of being loved and giving love?

12. If your child was a product of rape, how would you deal with the issue of telling your child without destroying his/her self-image? Do you think Haley's choice was the right one?

REQUEST YOUR FREE BOOKS!

2 FREE INSPIRATIONAL NOVELS
PLUS 2
FREE
MYSTERY GIFTS

LoveInspired

YES! Please send me 2 FREE Love Inspired® novels and my 2 FREE mystery gifts (gifts are worth about $10). After receiving them, if I don't wish to receive any more books, I can return the shipping statement marked "cancel". If I don't cancel, I will receive 4 brand-new novels every month and be billed just $4.24 per book in the U.S. or $4.74 per book in Canada, plus 25¢ shipping and handling per book and applicable taxes, if any*. That's a savings of over 20% off the cover price! I understand that accepting the 2 free books and gifts places me under no obligation to buy anything. I can always return a shipment and cancel at any time. Even if I never buy another book, the two free books and gifts are mine to keep forever.

113 IDN ERXA   313 IDN ERWX

Name   (PLEASE PRINT)

Address   Apt. #

City   State/Prov.   Zip/Postal Code

Signature (if under 18, a parent or guardian must sign)

Order online at www.LoveInspiredBooks.com

Or mail to Steeple Hill Reader Service:
IN U.S.A.: P.O. Box 1867, Buffalo, NY 14240-1867
IN CANADA: P.O. Box 609, Fort Erie, Ontario L2A 5X3
Not valid to current subscribers of Love Inspired books.

Want to try two free books from another series?
Call 1-800-873-8635 or visit www.morefreebooks.com

* Terms and prices subject to change without notice. N.Y. residents add applicable sales tax. Canadian residents will be charged applicable provincial taxes and GST. Offer not valid in Quebec. This offer is limited to one order per household. All orders subject to approval. Credit or debit balances in a customer's account(s) may be offset by any other outstanding balance owed by or to the customer. Please allow 4 to 6 weeks for delivery. Offer available while quantities last.

Your Privacy: Steeple Hill Books is committed to protecting your privacy. Our Privacy Policy is available online at www.SteepleHill.com or upon request from the Reader Service. From time to time we make our lists of customers available to reputable third parties who may have a product or service of interest to you. If you would prefer we not share your name and address, please check here.

LIREG08R

Love Inspired

TITLES AVAILABLE NEXT MONTH

Don't miss these four stories in January

ROCKY MOUNTAIN LEGACY by Lois Richer
Weddings by Woodwards

A bride should have a say in the most important day of her life, right? Not when her brother is Cade Porter. Star wedding planner Sara Woodward thinks Cade is too arrogant when he takes over his sister's wedding…until Cade assures Sara that when it comes to *their* wedding she's in control.

A FAMILY FOR LUKE by Carolyne Aarsen

A family is not something Luke Harris has ever had, and it's the only thing he wants. Yet his neighbor, overworked widow Janie Corbett, is sure this helpful man is too good to be true. With the help of Janie's three smart kids and one golden Labrador, they both may find that love lives right next door.

MOMMY'S HOMETOWN HERO by Merrillee Whren

The woman he's loved since childhood has finally returned to their small South Dakota town, and ex-soldier Matt Dalton is not giving her up without a fight. Single mom Rachel Charbonneau plans on leaving as soon as her family's farm is sold. Until Matt's love and faith make him her hometown hero.

DADDY FOR KEEPS by Pamela Tracy

One look in those green eyes and bull rider Lucas "Lucky" Welch knows the little boy in front of him is his late brother's son. Things get even more complicated as he learns the truth behind Robby's birth. Yet Lucky knows that if he hangs on tight he'll show Natalie Crosby that he can be not just a daddy but a husband for keeps.

LICNM1208BPA